# SHATTERED

## by Nigel Robinson

BOXTREE

First published in the UK 1993
by BOXTREE LIMITED, Broadwall House,
21 Broadwall, London SE1 9PL

10 9 8 7 6 5 4 3 2 1

The Fremantle Corporation, BAYWATCH™
is a trademark and © copyright 1993
The Baywatch Production Company

Cover and insert photographs: Kim Carlsberg
and Janet Makoska
Cover design by Nigel Davies at Titan Studio
1–85283–596–6

Phototypeset by Intype, London
Printed and bound by Cox & Wyman, Reading, Berkshire

A CIP catalogue entry for this book is available from the
British Library

# BAYWATCH™

# Prologue

Gary Russell stood on the top of the high rocky bank of the secluded cove, looked out to sea, and sighed. *Man there's no doubt about it*, he thought, *that ocean sure is something else*.

Before him, twinkling and sparkling in the early afternoon sunlight, was the largest, deepest, most beautiful and *bluest* ocean in the whole world. Gary knew that he was making the right choice when he'd booked this vacation to Southern California, and the sight of the magnificent Pacific Ocean merely confirmed his decision. It was a whole different ball game from the pollution and chaos and organised street crime of his home town of Detroit.

He turned back to help his girlfriend Hillary and her best pal, Morgan, down the steep bank to the tiny bay below. Gary had already taken down a small inflatable dinghy which was now waiting for them at the water's edge.

'Be careful,' Morgan said to Hillary as Gary helped his girlfriend down the slippery rocks.

'It's OK,' Hillary reassured her cautious friend. 'Follow me, there's nothing to worry about.'

'Oh yeah?' asked Morgan as she began her descent, clearly not believing her.

She paused and looked out to sea. Like Gary and Hillary, she also came from Detroit and this was her first trip down to the ocean: it seemed somehow fathomless and threatening, not at all like the inviting pictures she'd seen in the travel magazines or on the TV.

('Chill out!' Gary had told her when they were driving down here this morning. 'There's nothing to worry about. The Pacific's the most peaceful ocean in the world. That's why they named it *Pacific* isn't it?')

'Trust me!' urged Hillary.

*I trusted you about my blind date*, Morgan remembered grimly, and chuckled nervously: *And look who I got – the Hunchback of Notre Dame!*

'Watch your step, girls,' advised Gary, as he jumped off the rocks and on to the sand. 'It's a little slick here.' The rocks on the edge of the beach were razor-sharp: one slip and an unwary person from Detroit could easily cut his or her legs to ribbons.

When they were all safely down on the beach, Gary slung the backpack off his shoulder and threw it into the waiting dinghy. 'Come on,' he said, 'let's go.'

The two girls climbed in the dinghy after Gary, who pushed it away from the shore with a paddle. Hillary took the other paddle and they began to row out to their destination: a small rocky outcrop about fifty metres offshore. In fact, to call it even an outcrop was an exaggeration: it was little more than a large boulder jutting out of the smooth and silent waters of the Pacific.

But no matter what it was, no matter how big or how small it was, thought Gary, it was the perfect place for a picnic: isolated, sunny and set in the middle of the calmest, safest ocean in the entire world.

And he couldn't have been more wrong.

*

It took them about ten minutes to reach the small rock in the ocean and, as Hillary and Morgan clambered on to the outcrop and Gary moored the dinghy, they had to admit that he had been right all along. The water was so serene and calm out here; cut off as they were, they might have as well have been miles away from civilisation. In the distance they could see a school of porpoises playing in the sun-drenched waters, blissfully ignorant of the three humans on the rock.

'Isn't it beautiful!' Gary said as he joined them, perched on top of the outcrop. He glanced over at his rucksack which the girls had taken on to the rock. 'Well, c'mon, break open the wine!' he said. 'This is supposed to be a picnic!'

With a smile Hillary took a corkscrew from her bum-bag and uncorked the bottle of fine Californian Chablis.

'Look at those waves,' marvelled Gary as he opened the second bottle of wine some time later. The placid waters had now become slightly choppy and Morgan had noticed that the school of porpoises had vanished. 'Maybe tomorrow we should go surfing. They say Jimmy Slade, the guy in all the surf magazines, rides the waves round here. What's good enough for him . . .'

'This wind has really kicked up,' said Hillary. The ocean breeze was lashing her hair across her face.

'Are you sure we're OK up here?' Morgan asked nervously. She felt strangely unprotected here in the middle of the ocean, with the waves lapping at her feet as she dangled them off the edges of the rock.

Gary poured some more wine into her plastic cup. 'Relax, we're fine,' he insisted as he proffered it to her. 'Now have some wine and hang out, OK?'

Morgan nodded uncertainly and took the cup. By her side Hillary was lying flat out on the rock, soaking in the sun, and working on the perfect all-over Californian tan. Hey, she'd spent thousands on this vocation, so she was at least going to bring something back with her to Detroit.

Maybe it was the wine, or the warm sleepy rays of the sun, but soon they all dozed off. When Morgan awoke, about an hour later, the strong sea breeze had turned into a cold and biting wind. It hurled around the rock, churning the surface of the sea. In hardly any time at all the deceptively calm Pacific Ocean had reverted to its true nature.

Urgently Morgan, shook her two friends awake. The wind was stirring the sea into a turmoil, and bigger and bigger waves were crashing against the tiny rock on which they'd settled.

'We'd better get going, Gary,' said Hillary, as a particularly large wave crashed against their rock, drenching all three of them in spray.

'Hey, no biggie,' Gary said, clearly unfazed by the change in the Ocean. He stood up – rather shakily after the wine he had drunk – and pointed down to the dinghy which was moored by a length of rope to the rock. 'We've got our raft to take us back to land.'

Hillary stood up. 'Then we'd better get going,' she said. She tried to keep her voice steady but it was becoming difficult to conceal the fear she was now beginning to feel.

Gary coolly began to pack up their things and empty wine bottles into the backpack, when Morgan grabbed him by the arm.

'My God, Gary! Look! The boat!'

A particularly violent wave had smashed into the rock, tossing the dinghy in the air. With a dreadful *snap*! the dinghy loosed its mooring and was sent hurtling away into the wild waters of the Pacific. The current took it up, dragging it further and further away from them.

'Gary, go get it!' Hillary screamed hysterically. 'Get it back!'

Cursing under his breath, Gary jumped feet-first into the raging waters of the Pacific. With mighty strokes he propelled himself towards the quickly disappearing dinghy.

The dinghy moved inexorably away from Gary, as the ocean seemed to delight in toying with him like a cat would with a mouse. He would be within feet of the dinghy when a wave would suddenly smash into him, knocking him backwards, or a swell would rocket the dinghy even further away from him.

The wild waves of the Pacific crashed mercilessly into Gary, as his limbs ached and strained to keep himself afloat. But it was no use. No one, not even the strongest Olympic swimmer, would have been able to catch up with the speeding dinghy now.

Salt water stung his eyes, and he began to cough and splutter as one wave after another struck him with a force of which, a few hours ago, he would never have expected this 'peaceful' ocean to have been capable.

'Come back, Gary! Come back!' screamed Hillary and Morgan, as they stood on the rock, holding on to each other for balance.

Summoning up the last of his already battered energies, Gary turned and swam back to the rock where Hillary and Morgan managed to drag him, exhausted and sore, out of the churning waters and back on to the rock.

In the distance the dinghy was now little more than a tiny red speck bobbing along on the waves. And as it disappeared so did their only hope of making it back to land. None of

them would be able to swim the fifty metres or
so back to shore in these sorts of conditions.

Another wave crashed into the rock, almost
toppling Hillary. She fell to her knees and, with
aching fingers, clutched hold of the surface for
support.

'What are we going to do?' she screamed
above the noise of the waves 'We can't get back
to shore! Gary, do something! Do something!'

But Gary just looked at her with worried and
helpless eyes. There was nothing they could do.
They would never survive a swim back to shore
in those waters. And the tide was rising fast. It
looked as though they had only two options:
wait to be thrown off the rock by a strong wave,
or wait till the tide rose. Either way, they were
going to drown.

In – what had he called it? – in the most
peaceful ocean in the entire world.

# Chapter One

*Man, this is the life*, thought Mitch Buchannon, as he breathed the refreshing salt-tang of the breeze coming in from the Pacific Ocean, and stretched his arms wide as if to encompass the whole of Southern California.

This was what his life was all about, he decided: working down on the beach at Baywatch as one of the LA County Lifeguards, feeling the sand between his toes, the sun on his bronzed and muscled body.

He loved the team spirit of all the lifeguards working together under his charge, and the great surge of adrenalin when you're called out on a rescue mission. And then there was that irreplaceable feeling of being needed, that marvellous satisfaction when you know that you've

just saved someone's life: there was nothing in
the world which could match that sensation.

*Yes*, he decided. *The beach, this job, they're
what I live for. Baywatch is my home and my
whole world; and I don't know what I'd do if
anyone came along and took it away from me.*

And the perks were good too, he decided.
Here on the Californian beach the ocean was
the bluest, the surfing was the wildest, the
beach was the longest, and the girls! Well,
the girls just had to be the longest-legged, blon-
dest, sexiest bunch of chicks on the entire North
American Continent. And what was more, they
all thought the lifeguards working the beach
were pretty hot stuff as well.

*And hey, who am I to disappoint them?* he
grinned to himself, and continued chatting to a
group of cute tourists from Sacramento, who
had come down to Baywatch on their annual
vacation. They thought the life of a lifeguard
must be glamorous and exciting, and Mitch
wasn't going to contradict them. In fact, he was
bathing in all the adulation.

He felt a sharp tap on his shoulder and
turned around to see the figure of Stephanie
Holden, his fellow lieutenant on the beach. He
and Stephanie had once been a very serious
item, and even though that relationship had
long since ended they still remained the best of

friends. And what was more, she knew Mitch like no one else except his young son, Hobie.

'How's it going?' she asked.

Mitch looked guiltily at the gang of chattering, scantily-clad tourists, and then back at Stephanie. 'Well, it turned out to be a busy day...' he said sheepishly.

Stephanie gave Mitch a look which seemed to say: *Pull the other one, Buster! I wasn't born yesterday!*

'I can see that there's a lot here to keep your eye on,' she said sarcastically. *To be precise, three blondes, one brunette and one dazzling redhead who if she doesn't put more sun block on her lily-white skin is going to be lobster-red tomorrow,* she added to herself.

Mitch sniggered like a little boy caught doing something naughty – which is exactly what Stephanie considered him to be at that moment.

'Well, "keeping an eye on things" is part of our job description isn't it?'

Stephanie couldn't resist smiling too. She loved Mitch as a friend, and as an ex-lover, but there were times when she could quite cheerfully take him up to the top of a very high building and drop him off it, head first. This was one of those times.

'Well, when your "job" is over, and if you can tear yourself away,' she said, trying to sound

officious (and not succeeding), 'perhaps you'd
meet me up at headquarters.' She added point-
edly: 'That is, if you don't have any other
plans ...'

Mitch looked back at the girls, and shrugged
sadly: 'No. No plans yet ...'

'Great!' said Stephanie, and led Mitch to the
distinctive yellow transit truck of the LA
County Lifeguard. 'Because I have a stack of
incident reports that need filling out. And I'd
like you to join me!'

'Yeah ...' said Mitch with all the enthusiasm
of a nervous patient being shown into the den-
tist's surgery, and started to follow Stephanie
to the truck. He threw one final lingering and
regretful glance back at the girls. *Damn all that
paperwork!* he thought to himself.

                             *

Two hours later in the main operations room of
Baywatch headquarters, Mitch signed the final
one of his report sheets with a self-satisfied
flourish and filed the papers away in an official
folder. By his side Stephanie looked up jeal-
ously; she still had another twenty or so reports
to fill out.

'Why do you always finish your rescue reports
before I do?' she asked indignantly.

Mitch smiled smugly. 'I use smaller words,' he said. 'As a matter of fact, there's a very small word for what I'd like to do right now.' He looked meaningfully at his ex-lover.

Stephanie put down her pen; this sounded interesting. 'Animal, vegetable, or mineral?' she asked.

Mitch moved nearer to Stephanie and looked her directly in the eyes. Their faces drew closer. 'It's a little of all three,' he said suggestively.

Stephanie felt her pulse racing. Ever since they had gone on a cruise with the rest of the gang from Baywatch she had realised that there was still something between her and Mitch; was he really suggesting what she suspected? And even more importantly was that what she was hoping for?

'And what exactly do you have in mind?' she asked huskily.

Mitch pulled away suddenly. 'Eat!' he declared, and grinned at his joke. 'I'm starved – aren't you starved? Let's take a break!'

*Damn the man!* Stephanie cried. *He is completely and utterly impossible!*

'Trust a man to always be thinking about his stomach!' she chided.

'Not always,' Mitch said, and winked even more meaningfully at her. He stood up to make his way to the canteen when the phone on the desk rang. He picked up the receiver.

'Baywatch. Buchannon speaking.' By his side Stephanie saw Mitch's face suddenly turn serious: something was up.

'Where? How many?' Mitch snapped into the phone. 'OK, we're on our way!' He replaced the receiver and marched to the door with Stephanie in hot pursuit. 'C'mon, Steph, let's roll,' he said.

'Where to?'

'The bluff at Point Dume.' He turned to Ben, one of the radio operators at headquarters, a middle-aged man who needed a cane to help him walk. 'Ben – ' he looked at the roster sheet on the wall which displayed the names of the on-duty lifeguards – 'get Newman and Barnett on the horn and tell them to meet us in the garage in five minutes.'

'Will do,' said Ben, and was already making the connection. In the old days he'd too been a lifeguard: he recognised the urgency in Mitch's voice.

'Mitch, what's up?' asked Stephanie as she followed him out of headquarters.

'I'll tell you on the way!' he said, and ran down to the garage, taking the steps two at a time as usual.

# Chapter Two

Sirens blaring, the two yellow Baywatch rescue vehicles screeched to a halt on Point Dume bluff. Mitch and Stephanie leapt out of the first one and ran over to the local sheriff who was looking out to sea. They were followed in the second truck by Newman and Barnett, two other lifeguards at Baywatch.

'What's happened?' Mitch asked the sheriff.

The sheriff pointed out to the rocky outcrop, from which Gary, Hillary and Morgan were frantically waving and shouting. The tide had risen to cover most of the outcrop; they were huddled together at the very summit of the rock.

'I saw them by chance when I spotted their trailer parked illegally,' he said. 'I don't know how long they've been down there, but the tide is rising fast.'

Mitch shaded his eyes from the sun and quickly assessed the situation. The sea was getting rougher by the minute and only a strong and trained swimmer would be able to swim over to the reef without being smashed against the rocks of the bay.

As the sheriff had said, the tide was rising fast: Mitch estimated that the three on the rock had just under another fifteen minutes before the water covered them completely.

He turned briskly back to the rescue vehicle and took out a rubber wetsuit which he began to clamber into.

'Radio the paramedics,' he ordered the sheriff. 'Tell them we're going to need back-up.' If the guys out on the rock had been in the water for any length of time they would be freezing by now, in spite of the warm rays of the Californian sun; shock could also set in which would make their rescue even more difficult and hazardous. Gary and his friends were going to need all the medical help they could muster.

Stephanie and Newman had already changed into wetsuits and were carrying their buoyant rescue cans down the steep bluff face which led to the water's edge. The rocks here were razor-sharp and brutal, Stephanie realised, and could

cut an unwary swimmer to pieces; it was for
that very reason, and for the unpredictable
nature of this part of the ocean, that even professional swimmers and surfers avoided Point
Dume.

'Hook up the rescue basket,' Mitch instructed
Barnett who was to stay on the shore. If any of
the guys on the rock were injured they might
be unable to climb up to safety; Barnett would
then use the rescue basket to hoist them up the
side of the bluff.

Stephanie and Newman were already in the
water, hurtling towards the outcrop with strong
and sure strokes. They trailed behind them
their red rescue cans; these buoyancy aids
would help Gary, Hillary and Morgan to stay
afloat when they dragged them back to land.
Mitch ran in after them, and soon caught up
with them.

The wind was howling now, churning and
tossing the sea even more. Huge waves
smashed relentlessly into the three lifeguards
as they made their way through the water to
the rock.

Most of it was now covered: the water had
reached Gary, Hillary and Morgan's waists, and
they were holding on for grim life. Even above
the crashing roar of the ocean Mitch and the
others could hear their hysterical screams.

Muscles straining and their eyes stinging from the salt water, the three lifeguards finally reached the outcrop. Newman swam over to where Gary was straining to hold on to the rock. His fingers were torn and bloodied, shreds of flesh ripped away by the rocks he had been battered against.

'I got ya!' Newman cried above the noise of the waves, and grabbed hold of Gary, who was still holding on tightly to the outcrop.

'Let go,' Newman urged. 'Just trust me!'

As gently as he could in the churning waters, Newman eased Gary off the rock, putting his arm around Gary's neck so that he could draw him back to shore doing the backstroke, keeping the young man's head above water all the time. With the added buoyancy of the rescue can – and provided Gary remained calm and didn't panic – it would be a relatively easy operation to get him back safely.

Near him, Stephanie had already taken hold of Morgan and was pushing them both off the rocky outcrop. With determined forceful strokes, she made her way back to shore.

Now only Hillary was left on the rock. She was paralysed with fear, shaking convulsively, as Mitch swam round to her.

'C'mon, trust me,' he said softly.

Hillary shook her head: she had been terri-

fied of water all her life and had never learnt
to swim.

'No-no-no, I can't, I can't,' she sobbed.

'Just let go of the rock and come to me,' he
urged. 'You'll be perfectly safe . . .'

'No-no-no, I can't, I can't, I can't . . .'

Hillary was close to hysteria, Mitch realised,
and would never leave the rock unless he dragged her off it physically. He pulled himself up
on to the rock, and handed her his rescue can.

'Grab my can and I'll swim you in,' he said.
'You'll be all right. OK?'

Hillary looked at the choppy waters of the
Pacific.

The biggest, *deepest* ocean in the world, Gary
had called it.

'No, I can't make it! I can't make it!'

Suddenly the mighty Pacific decided to take
matters into its own hands. A massive wave
washed over them, sweeping them off the rock
and into the sea. Hillary started to scream as
she felt herself being dragged under by the
ocean's greedy currents. Mitch grabbed her and
began to pull her to shore.

Hillary was in a fit of blind, unthinking panic
now. She was kicking out in a desperate
attempt to keep her head above water, not
realising that if she would only remain calm
Mitch and the rescue can would easily keep her

afloat. She lashed out at Mitch, who needed all his strength to restrain her, as he slowly drew her shorewards.

'Hang on!' he said to her as they approached the bluff. She was still thrashing wildly about in the water. 'You're almost home now.'

On the bluff Gary and Morgan were waiting for them, wrapped in towels to keep them warm. Barnett was down at the bottom of the bluff, at the water's edge. He reached out his hands as Mitch and Hillary approached them.

'Come on!' shouted Mitch to Hillary, struggling to make himself heard above the noise of the waves and Hillary's own hysterical screams. 'Go grab a hold of him!'

Barnett reached down, and hauled the shaking and sobbing Hillary out of the shallows.

Still in the water Mitch relaxed, relieved that another tricky rescue had gone more or less according to plan. In doing so, he let his guard drop for one vital half-instant.

Barnett saw it first, as he helped Hillary back up the bluff face. He screamed out a warning.

'Mitch! Look out! A wave!'

The warning came too late. The enormous wave bore down on Mitch with a stomach-churning force, and lifted him in the air, tossing him like a top. Helpless, he was swept along in its course, heading directly towards the bluff face.

Mitch was smashed against the rock; he cried out in agony as every single bone in his body seemed to shatter. Pain coursed through all his limbs, a sharp deadly pain that was almost too much to bear. The world turned a sickening red before his eyes, and he started to lose consciousness.

He shook himself awake, as yet another wave came down on him and thudded him like a helpless rag doll once more against the cliff wall. And another. And, relentlessly, brutally another. He tried vainly to swim away from the oncoming waves, but the Pacific Ocean had him in its grasp now, and like a rabid dog, just wouldn't let go.

Blood streamed out of Mitch's mouth, and choking sea water poured into his lungs, as he struggled desperately to breathe. A cloud descended upon him, and the water suddenly felt agonisingly, deadly cold.

His vision blurred, and faltered, and went, and Mitch lost consciousness.

*

Mitch came to, and for a moment thought it had all been a bad dream. Then dreadful reality dawned and he realised that he was still in the water. Stephanie's arms were around him.

'Mitch! Mitch!' she called, shaking him to full consciousness. 'I've got you, you'll be OK.'

As soon as she had seen the big wave coming, Stephanie had raced down the bluff face into the water. Now she was holding Mitch afloat, and slowly swimming with him towards a calmer part of the bay.

Still weak and winded from the assault by the waves, Mitch tried to swim alongside Stephanie. His face turned white with fear.

'My legs!' he cried. 'I can't move my legs!' He started to panic, before he remembered the cardinal rule of lifesaving: when you panic you only make the lifeguard's task more difficult. He struggled to remain calm, as Stephanie towed him back to the shore.

At the water's edge Barnett and Newman were waiting anxiously for them. Above them on the bluff the team of paramedics had arrived.

'It's his back,' Stephanie called out to her fellow lifeguards, as they ran into the water to help them out. 'Don't lift his legs! He can't move his legs!'

Barnett ran back up the bluff to collect the backboard which was a standard part of any lifeguard's rescue equipment, and to alert the paramedics.

Newman splashed through the water to Stephanie and Mitch's side. 'Keep on his head!' he said, ordering Stephanie to hold Mitch's head steady in her hands: if his back had been broken . . .

Mitch looked up helplessly at his old friend. 'Newman, I can't . . . I can't . . .' he croaked.

'You're gonna be fine, Mitch, old buddy,' he said, as Barnett returned with the backboard. 'OK, Mitch, we're gonna get you on a backboard now. Easy does it . . .'

Gently Stephanie, Newman and Barnett rolled Mitch on to the backboard. Mitch clenched his teeth, trying not to scream, as shafts of pain ripped through his body like red-hot needles. Shot throughout his whole body – apart from his legs. Above them, the paramedic team was already lowering the rescue basket which they would use to haul Mitch up to the top of the bluff.

'Did the girl make it?' Mitch asked Stephanie, who was still holding his head tight, until the paramedics could get down and fasten a neck brace.

'Yes,' she whispered. 'Don't talk: save your energy.'

Stephanie was close to tears now, but was restraining to keep her voice steady for Mitch's benefit. *Please God*, she kept repeating to herself like a mantra. *Please let him be all right. Just let him be all right!*.

'I gotta write the incident report...' Mitch said.

'Don't worry,' said Stephanie, as the paramedics arrived and began to lower down the rescue basket.

'I'll write up the report ... I'll even use smaller words ...' This time she couldn't contain her emotions and the tears flowed freely from her eyes.

The paramedics had reached Mitch and Stephanie now and were busy strapping Mitch's limbs together, to ensure that he couldn't move and exacerbate any injuries he might have sustained. As gently as they could, they placed him in the rescue basket which they then slowly hoisted up to the top of the bluff. Stephanie clambered up to the top and had already opened the ambulance door by the time Mitch had been pulled up.

'I'm riding with him,' she told Barnett and Newman. 'You two can fill out the incident report.'

As the ambulance sped away, its sirens blaring, Barnett and Newman began to quiz Gary, Hillary and Morgan on what they were doing on the rock in the first place. Barnett and Newman were trained professionals, but even so it was difficult to conceal the anger and ill will they felt towards Gary and his two friends. After all, their irresponsible little jaunt might just have ended forever the career of the best damn life-guard Baywatch had ever known.

# Chapter Three

Stephanie breezed cheerfully into the hospital room, carrying a huge vase of flowers to add to the ones which the guys at Baywatch had already sent Mitch. Mitch was lying on the bed, still in traction, although he could now move his head. By his bedside was Hobie, his eleven-year-old son from his marriage; his large brown eyes were full of concern for his father, whom he treated as his very best buddy.

'I'm taking care of everything at your house,' Stephanie said, as she arranged the flowers. 'Hobie's doing all his homework – and I'm doing all the cooking.'

Hobie nodded. 'She even burned a few things so that we wouldn't miss you so much,' he quipped and then was suddenly serious again. 'Dad, are you really OK?'

'Sure I am.'

Hobie held his father's hand. 'Dad, I'm gonna take care of you until you get better,' he declared. 'I promise.'

A look passed between Mitch and Stephanie, a grown-up look which Hobie didn't notice, so concerned was he for his father's welfare.

'Well, he's gonna be better real soon,' said Stephanie, hoping she sounded convincing enough. 'So you'd better enjoy taking care of your dad while you can.'

There was a knock on the door and Doctor Bonann, a grey-haired reliable man in his early sixties, entered. He was the doctor who had been assigned to Mitch's case.

'Good morning.'

'Morning, Doctor,' said Mitch and noticed the clipboard the white-coated doctor was carrying under his arm. 'You got my test results.'

Bonann nodded, and then looked meaningfully at Stephanie and Hobie. Stephanie got the hint and started to hustle Hobie out of the room. 'Let's give your dad a little time with the doctor, shall we?' she suggested.

'But I want to stay with him!'

'Hobie, it's OK,' said Mitch, anxious that his son shouldn't hear the bad news the doctor might have in store for him. 'You can come back here before the doctor leaves.'

Hobie resigned himself to the inevitable and allowed Stephanie to usher him out of the room, leaving Mitch alone with Bonann.

'Mitch, I know that this must be the longest day of your life,' he began, 'so I'll cut right to the chase.'

Mitch looked the doctor firmly in the eyes. 'Why do I have the feeling that this isn't gonna be good news?' he asked gloomily.

The doctor consulted the results of Mitch's tests which were on the clipboard.

'Your X-rays and your MRI indicate that there are no breaks along the vertebrae, so that's good news, at least,' he said.

'But?'

'But you do have some serious damage to your spinal cord . . .'

'What kind of damage?' Mitch demanded urgently. He felt his heart beginning to pound with apprehension. And cold fear.

'When your back was thrown up against the rocks – while nothing was broken – the compression that it caused left bruising, which in turn caused swelling. That's why you have no feeling below your waist . . .'

Mitch frowned, unsure what to think. It didn't sound too serious: just a little swelling. So why was the doctor looking like he'd pronounced someone's death sentence?

'How long will it take for the swelling to go down?' he asked.

'It may be some time . . .' Bonann said slowly. 'And you'll need rehabilitation and physiotherapy. And time . . .'

Mitch took a deep breath. There was one question he had to know the answer to. And it was going to take a helluva lot of courage to ask it.

'But I am – I am – I am gonna walk again, aren't I?'

The doctor shrugged. 'I wish I could give you some guarantees, Mitch, but there are no guarantees,' he said sadly. He adopted a businesslike manner again. 'Now, as soon as you're able I'm going to transfer you to a rehabilitation centre. And I can't stress enough that physiotherapy is absolutely crucial if you're ever going to walk again.'

But Mitch was no longer listening. He seemed to be a long way off, looking down on himself, immobile and helpless in his hospital bed. The doctor was talking to someone else, wasn't he? He wasn't talking to Mitch Buchannon; it wasn't Mitch Buchannon who had just been told that he might never walk again.

Mitch felt the blood thunder in his ears and there was a cold sweat on his brow. Playing over and over and over again in his mind were

Doctor Bonann's words, words which had just changed his entire life.

*There are no guarantees, Mitch. No guarantees, no guarantees . . .*

*

Stephanie and Hobie looked up anxiously as Doctor Bonann left Mitch's room. They had been sitting for the past fifteen minutes in a small waiting area, just around the corner from Mitch's room. Stephanie nudged Hobie.

'It looks like the doctor's through,' she said. 'You can go and see your dad now.'

Hobie needed no further encouragement and walked off towards Mitch's room, waving hello to the doctor on the way. As the doctor passed her by Stephanie stood up and called him over. There was a deeply concerned expression on her face.

'Doctor Bonann,' she began tentatively. 'I want to know the truth.'

The doctor considered. Normally only next-of-kin would be allowed the full details of a patient's case. But he had seen the way Mitch and Stephanie had looked at each other in the hospital room, and also the rapport that Stephanie had with Mitch's son. Finally he decided that, with the exception of Hobie, Stephanie

Holden was the closest person in Mitch's life at
the moment. She deserved to be made aware of
all the facts.

'What are the chances?' Stephanie persisted.

'For a full recovery?' Stephanie nodded and
Bonann continued: 'The most important thing
is a positive mental attitude. If patients knew
the odds they were facing then they could easily
give up before they started.'

'And what are the odds?' Stephanie
demanded: no matter how it hurt she still had
to know.

'With the lumbar compression I'd say the
odds for a full recovery are about five per
cent . . .'

'*Five per cent?*'

For Stephanie the prospect couldn't bear
being thought about. Mitch, always so dynamic,
so active, so alive, had a one-in-twenty chance
of walking again?

'I can't . . . I can't believe that Mitch might
never walk again . . .'

'So don't believe it,' said Bonann, almost chal-
lengingly. Stephanie looked curiously at the
doctor as he continued: 'Mitch is going to need
all the support and encouragement and positive
energy that you can give him.'

Stephanie nodded. Mitch had stood by her in

the past when the going had been tough; now it was her turn to help him.

But as Doctor Bonann walked away she felt the tears well up in her eyes. *If Mitch is feeling even half as devastated as I am now, then he must be feeling terrible!* Ignoring the curious stares of passers-by she allowed her tears to flow freely.

Unknown to her, just around the corner, Hobie too was weeping silent tears. He had heard the entire conversation between Stephanie and the doctor.

*Dad not walking again? That's gonna destroy his life, it's gonna kill him,* Hobie realised.

*We've all gotta be strong for him now. Dad's gonna need me now like he's never done before,* Hobie told himself, *And I'm not gonna let him down!*

# Chapter Four

The West Hills Rehabilitation Center is one of the best hospitals in Southern California with a reputation second to none. It specialises in the care and rehabilitation of people who have been injured or crippled in accidents, and provides all the facilities needed for getting people back on their feet as quickly as possible: weights rooms, swimming pools, even a basketball court where wheelchair-bound residents whizz around the asphalt just as speedily as any Harlem Globetrotter.

The patients at West Hills cover the entire age range, from seventy-year-olds who may have injured their hip in a nasty fall, to young kids, mowed down on the highway by manic and drunken car drivers.

One of the youngest was just arriving at the

Center, a chirpy black boy, about eleven years
old. He was being pushed in his wheelchair by
a pretty young nurse who was all teeth and
smiles.

'Now, Jason,' she said brightly, 'there's a lot
of kids here your own age, so I think you're
gonna like it here, OK?'

Jason didn't say anything, just stared at her
from beneath the rim of his Chicago Bears baseball cap. *What did she know?* he asked himself.
*She can walk right out of here whenever she
wants. But me, hey, I'm never gonna walk again!*

And then Jason sniggered to himself, as he
looked around at the plush reception area into
which she wheeled him. *Quite a classy joint*, he
remarked to himself, as he saw the smart
leather seats, the enormous potted palms and
ferns, the state-of-the-art computer check-in
system, and the pretty young nurses in their
crisply starched white uniforms.

*Not bad for a black kid from Chicago, whose
mom's on welfare*, he thought. *And I'm even
getting it all for free! What would the nurse say
if she knew the real reason I've been brought
here!*

Watching the nurse check in Jason at the
reception desk was a bespectacled silver-haired
doctor, and a burly man dressed in an ill-fitting
suit. He had an untidy moustache and the

sweat on his brow showed that he was more used to the cooler temperatures of Chicago than the often stifling heat of Southern California. He looked like a cop from a second-rate TV series, and a cop is precisely what he was.

'I spent a year working on this case, Doctor Zack,' he said to his companion.

Doctor Zack was intrigued: he knew that there was something special about Jason – after all, eleven-year-olds from downtown Chicago weren't usually flown to Southern California, even though his hospital was widely known as one of the best on the West Coast. He asked the burly detective for more details.

'Jason took a bullet in the spine, trying to protect his older brother,' he explained. 'His brother was mixed up with a gang and when a drug deal went down, well, Jason's brother didn't make it . . . Jason is my only witness.'

Zack nodded sympathetically. 'That's an awful lot for a boy that age to go through, Detective North,' he said. 'The murder of his brother – and a forthcoming trial.'

'The trial's still a month away,' said Detective North. 'I brought him here from Chicago to keep him safe.'

Zack looked reprovingly at North. 'Mr North, this is a rehabilitation hospital: it is not a safe house.'

'He needs *both* facilities right now, Doc,' North insisted, and added: 'No-one but you and I know who he is, and why he's here. We've got to keep that secret. There are people out there who wouldn't think twice about killing Jason to get themselves off the rap . . .'

\*

Following Jason up the ramp leading to the reception area were Mitch, Stephanie and Hobie. Stephanie was pushing Mitch in a wheelchair of which he was an obviously extremely reluctant occupant. Mitch hated being out of control like this, hated being dependent on anyone, even on Stephanie. He was used to people needing him, not the other way round.

'I'm gonna get us checked in,' Stephanie said brightly and walked off towards the reception desk. Hobie mumbled that he was going to the vending machine at the far end of the room to buy something to eat.

When they had gone, Mitch looked around at the other people in reception. There were people in wheelchairs like himself, people on crutches and others moving around with the help of zimmer frames. The white-coated nurses, were dashing about flitting from one urgent task to another and, to Mitch, just cruelly emphasising his own immobility.

*Hell, I should be up and about*, he thought angrily, *not being wheeled around like – like some damn cripple!*

His heart sank as he realised that, for the moment at least, a cripple was exactly what he was.

'Here, kitty, kitty, kitty . . .'

Mitch turned around to see a young black boy in a wheelchair clucking away at a small kitten, which had taken up residence underneath one of the leather sofas lining the walls of the reception area. The boy was too small to reach down and pick up the kitten; the animal was too shy and wary to come up to the boy.

Mitch smiled wryly to himself. At last he could be of some use! Sure, it wasn't on a par with saving lives out there at Baywatch but what the hell!

He wheeled himself over awkwardly – he still hadn't quite got the hang of operating his wheelchair yet – and reached down and picked up the kitten.

'Here's your little friend for you,' Mitch said, as he passed the purring kitten over to Jason, whose face lit up.

'Gee thanks,' Jason said gratefully.

'Hey, no problem,' said Mitch who was

already warming to the young boy. He winked mischievously at him. 'Maybe you and I can have a drag race in our wheelchairs some day, huh?'

Jason nodded enthusiastically; there might not be many advantages to being confined to a wheelchair, but it sure was fun racing down the corridors of a hospital scaring the life out of any nurse who happened to get in your way!

Doctor Zack came up behind Jason and gave Mitch a nod of welcome. 'Come on, Jason, let me take you to your room, OK?'

Jason muttered his reluctant assent and allowed himself to be taken to the elevator to his private room on the second floor. The elevator doors slid open and a tall black woman marched out.

She was in her late twenties, with a trendily short hair cut, and was wearing an equally trendy blouse and black Lycra leggings. She looked around the reception area, and then caught sight of Mitch in his wheelchair. His eyes lit up and she strode purposefully over to him.

'My God, are you a handsome hunk or what!' she said in a voice as loud and as flamboyant as the multi-coloured top she was wearing.

At the reception desk Stephanie giggled, assuming the woman to have just come from visiting one of the patients. Aware that all eyes were on him, the embarrassed Mitch looked around as if to say: *Does she mean me?*

The woman stood back and inspected Mitch, sizing him up. She nodded approvingly and then announced: 'Let me tell you now, honey, I am gonna do everything I can to get you up and out of that chair – 'cause I wanna see those cute buns of yours up and movin'! She held out her hand for Mitch to shake. 'I'm Sophie Jones.'

Mitch took her proffered hand. 'Hi, and I'm . . .'

'Honey, there ain't a person here in this hospital – well, unless he's in a coma, that is – that doesn't know who you are!' she gushed. 'You are a hero! Can I call you Mitch?'

Mitch shrugged, embarrassed by all the unwelcome attention the vociferous Sophie was drawing to them.

'Sure,' he said in response to Sophie's question, 'that's my name!'

Sophie beamed, and Stephanie and Hobie came over for Mitch to introduce them. Sophie regarded Hobie with the same studied appreciation she had given Mitch.

'Well, it sure is a pleasure meeting you, Hobie,' she gushed once more, and ruffled his brown hair. 'I'm speaking on behalf of all the women on this planet when I tell you don't go breaking our hearts, OK?'

'I won't,' Hobie promised, and couldn't resist grinning. There was something incredibly likeable about this woman with the voice as loud as a foghorn, and all the innate over-the-top exuberance of a Children's TV presenter. Even Stephanie found herself warming to the bouncy black woman: she couldn't imagine anyone ever resisting Sophie's charms and enthusiasm: it would be a little bit like trying to stand up to a tornado.

'Have you all been taken care of?' Sophie asked.

Stephanie nodded. 'We're all checked in,' she confirmed. 'We're just waiting for the physiotherapist.'

'Then wait no longer!' Sophie announced, and turned back to Mitch. There was a brilliant smile on her face. 'Honey, you now have your own personal gym teacher!'

Mitch's face fell. Just when he was at his lowest ebb he was going to have to contend with someone who probably possessed all the energy needed to light up the whole of downtown Los Angeles?

'*You're* my physiotherapist?' he asked in disbelief.

'And aren't you the lucky one!'

David Hasselhoff plays Mitch Buchannon

On set: filming the episode *Strangers*. From
left to right: David Hasselhoff, Jeremy Jackson
and Pamela Anderson

Pamela Anderson plays C. J. Parker

David Charvet as Matt Brody

Alexandra Paul plays Stephanie Holden

Nicole Eggert relaxing off-set

Jeremy Jackson plays with a puppy

The *Baywatch* team in relaxed mode. From left to right: Nicole Eggert, David Hasselhoff, Jeremy Jackson, Alexandra Paul, David Charvet and Pamela Anderson

Beside Mitch's wheelchair, Stephanie laughed silently to herself. Since the accident Mitch had been listless and depressed, quite understandably so. If anyone was going to put some enthusiasm and the spark of life in him, if anyone was going to get him back on his feet and walking again, then that someone was going to be Sophie Jones!

*

Outside in a telephone booth in the hospital car park, where he couldn't be heard, Detective North dialled a long-distance number. He tapped anxiously on the glass of the booth as the connection was made over two-and-a-half thousand miles.

In a cramped office in Chicago Detective Ruddick, North's immediate superior picked up the phone. A square-jawed, handsome thirty-something who always dressed impeccably in designer clothes (even though he was only on a cop's salary), he was in charge of the operation to crack down on the gangsters who had shot Jason's brother dead.

North's voice came crackling down over the line: 'I've got our witness tucked away safe and sound in a rehab centre.'

At his desk Ruddick grabbed a pencil. 'Where are you?' he asked urgently.

'LA,' answered North. 'I'm not taking any chances this time. If we nail these gangsters who wasted the kid's brother, then they'll hand us their suppliers on a silver platter.'

'You're doing a great job, Sam,' Ruddick congratulated him. 'Now where in LA are you?' He scribbled down the address on a scrap of paper. 'Thanks, Sam, great work!' he finished and put down the phone.

He reached out instantly for the second phone on his desk, the one which had a direct line that didn't go through the switchboard where calls were logged. He stabbed out a local number on the keyboard; the call was answered instantly.

'It's Ruddick here,' he said. 'North has the kid stashed away in some rehab centre out in LA . . . I'm on my way . . . And don't worry – I'll make it look like an accident . . .'

# Chapter Five

The following morning Sophie cheerfully pushed Mitch's wheelchair down the long, winding corridors of West Hills. Mitch was beginning to tire of Sophie's constant optimism and happy manner; he felt resentful that she was walking while he wasn't and had been particularly grumpy all morning. His ill humour had had no effect on Sophie whatsoever: she'd been doing her job for years and understood the initial emotional pain and trauma people went through when they were brought to the Centre for the first time. Mitch was proving no more difficult than any other of her charges: and most of them were now up and walking.

Sophie planned to spend the morning introducing Mitch to some of his fellow patients, and get him acquainted with some of the facilities

the centre had on offer, which included a small
gym (*a gym for people who can't walk*? Mitch
had thought. *What crazy dumb-ass notion is
that*?) and a pool.

'Swimming ought to make you feel right at
home, Mitch,' she breezed. 'Were you ever in
the armed services?'

'The Navy Seals,' he replied.

'Navy Seals, huh?' she said, and briskly
turned a corner. 'Sounds like some kind of
summer camp!'

'Summer camp?' Mitch repeated, and gave a
wry smile. 'I suppose it was – it was the most
gruelling thing I've ever been through – '

'You mean until now!' Sophie said, as she
pushed open the double doors which led into
the gym.

The air was alive with the grunts and moans
of people lifting free weights or working out at
the multi-gym machines, exercising every part
of their body. Each patient had his or her own
personal gym teacher, who guided them
through every part of their exercises, which
were designed to build and strengthen muscles
which might have been wasted through lack of
use. So determined were they all that none
of them looked up when Sophie and Mitch
entered.

Sophie looked down at Mitch. 'Well, are you

ready to begin?' she asked. Her tone was much
more serious now, as she realised what Mitch
was going through.

Mitch regarded the people in the gym with
an almost frightened look in his eyes. There
were people here who, like him, couldn't walk
and they were lying face down on workout
benches while their personal trainers manipu-
lated and massaged their legs, trying to raise
some feeling or movement.

Over there was a young mother, recently crippled in a road accident, who had just been told
that she would never walk again; she was sitting on a bench performing a series of dumbell
curls; a young man, whose legs had been
crushed in an industrial accident, was at the
pec-deck, grunting as he performed a series of
flies.

*All of them disabled and crippled*, realised
Mitch. *And I'm just like them!*

'Are you ready?' Sophie repeated.

Mitch shook his head. 'I don't know.'

'Mitch,' Sophie began sternly, 'if you want to
get up and out of this chair then there is absolutely no room for any self-pity.'

Mitch eyed Sophie knowingly. She understood too much, he decided. She understood
how easy it would be to remain in this wheel-

chair, to give up the struggle to walk again before he had even started.

*Yeah, she's a clever one, all right*, he thought. *And I'm not gonna give her the satisfaction of seeing me beat!*

'All right,' he shrugged. 'Let's give it a try . . .'

Sophie beamed. 'Now you are talkin' my language, sugar!' She turned to the group and clapped her hands to get their attention. 'Hi, everybody!' she shouted, and gestured to Mitch in his wheelchair beside her. 'This is Mitch!'

The others responded with muttered greetings of 'Hi, Mitch!' and then went back to their workouts.

'Mitch, this is everybody,' said Sophie. 'Don't worry, you'll meet them all again in the therapy sessions.'

She wheeled Mitch over to a pair of dumbbells. Although getting Mitch's legs to work again was her prime responsibility, it was also necessary to ensure that he kept the rest of his body in tip-top shape while he was immobile.

As Mitch began a series of bicep curls, Sophie watched encouragingly.

'You've got a lot of work to do here, Mitch,' she said. 'But it's all gonna pay off.' She turned Mitch's face to look at hers and fixed him with a steely and determined stare. 'Because you are gonna walk out of here!'

*

By the end of the day Mitch's body was aching all over; except, he reflected sadly, his legs which still had no feeling whatsoever. After the gruelling workout which Sophie had put him through, they had spent another hour manipulating and massaging his legs, trying to get some feeling and movement back into them.

A short, high-protein lunch, and then it was back to the gym again, before taking a dip in the therapy pool. This was a small pool into which Mitch was lowered by means of a chair attached to a pulley system. Water therapy was essential for rehabilitation, and, although Mitch could swim a few yards without using his legs, the water's natural buoyancy didn't help in getting his legs to move.

This was perhaps the most galling part of the day for Mitch. Not being able to walk on dry land was one thing, but being helpless in the water was another even more hurtful thing. Mitch had always been an expert swimmer and the rows of awards and plaques which lined the walls of his home at Baywatch were proof of that, but now he couldn't even move a few feet without assistance. He felt like a wretched baby, dependent on its mother and not able to fend for himself.

Following the hour in the therapy pool, Mitch had another hour of one-to-one counselling with Sophie. Sophie was convinced that Mitch was going to be able to walk again and she countered each and every one of Mitch's fears with well thought-out and reasoned arguments. After all, what Mitch was going through was nothing new.

When Mitch had finished his therapy chat with Sophie it was time for another hour in the gym, where Sophie put him through his paces again. In the gym Sophie was a slave-driver, forcing him to do one more set of reps, urging him to try and lift just one more heavier weight.

By the time the communal evening meal was over Mitch was exhausted. He looked at his watch: it was only 9.30 but he was so tired that all he wanted to do now was hit the sack and fall asleep.

As he wheeled himself down the darkened and empty corridor to the elevator he started. Before him was an overturned wheelchair, and slumped beside it the figure of a small boy.

Mitch automatically tried to leap out of his chair to run towards the boy, and cursed under his breath when his legs failed to respond. Grabbing hold of the wheels of his chair, he sped to the boy's side.

Mitch breathed a sigh of relief when he saw

that Jason was unhurt. Beside the lad on the
ground was a pack of about forty brightly coloured baseball cards, each one bearing the portrait of a member of the baseball hall of fame.
It was obvious that Jason had dropped one of
the cards and, in reaching over to pick it up,
had lost his balance and fallen out of his wheelchair. With his legs just as useless as Mitch's
there was no way he could get back into his
chair without assistance.

Mitch grinned down at Jason. 'Hey, you OK,
partner?' he asked cheerfully.

'Can you get my cards for me?' he said, and
Mitch began to help him collect the scattered
cards together.

'What happened?' Mitch asked. 'Were you
drag racing without me?'

Jason shrugged and grinned back cheekily.
As far as he was concerned falling out of your
wheelchair was no great shakes; picking up his
baseball cards was, however.

'I guess so,' he replied. 'I was just going too
fast . . .'

'By the way, I never introduced myself: I'm
Mitch,' he said.

'Everyone knows who you are,' said Jason.
'You're the big hero.'

Mitch blushed with embarrassment again.
'What's your name?'

The lad hesitated for a moment – *Was there something wrong*? Mitch wondered – before replying: 'Jason.'

'Nice to meet you, Jason,' he said, and offered the boy his arm, pulling him back up into his chair. For the first time since he had lost all feeling in his legs Mitch felt of use again: it was good to be helping someone else.

\*

Within days Mitch and Jason had become the best of buddies. Jason reminded Mitch a lot of Hobie, and although his son and Stephanie came to visit him every day, along with some of the other guys from Baywatch, it was still good to have a friend to chat to all through the day and to play card games with until late at night – or, at least, until Jason's bedtime.

Sophie looked on approvingly as the two friends sat outside in the warm sunshine on the lawn in front of the Rehabilitation Center. Jason was good for Mitch, she realised, keeping the lifeguard's mind off his problems. More importantly the feisty youngster was a fighter and an inspiration to Mitch.

'These are the best candy bars,' Jason confided in Mitch, and pulled two bars of chocolate from the pocket of his hooded sweatshirt. 'The

nurse keeps them behind her desk in the lobby.'
He offered Mitch a piece.

'Now I know two things about you,' Mitch
said as he munched on the piece of candy. 'You
like candy bars and baseball cards.'

Jason's face became even more animated as
the conversation once again turned to his
favourite topic. It was the one great passion of
his life, and he knew everything there was to
know about the game.

He pulled out the pack of cards which he
always carried around with him, and showed
them to Mitch.

'This is my most valuable one,' he said, showing Mitch a card with the picture of a baseball
player, his bat raised and ready to strike the
ball. 'Ken Griffee Junior. It's his rookie.'

'Wow!' said Mitch, only half-seriously. He'd
liked baseball at high school but his favourite
sports had always been swimming and kayak-
ing, and his heroes Olympic record-breakers.

Jason pulled another card from out of the
pack; this card was a little dog-eared and had
obviously been lovingly handled many times.

'Now this is a Ted Williams card,' Jason
explained, referring to the near-legendary Californian hitter who played for the Boston Red
Sox. He frowned: 'It's OK, but not as valuable
as one autographed by Ted Williams.'

'Oh,' said Mitch, trying to sound suitably interested and impressed.

'My brother was saving up to buy me one just before . . .' Jason's voice trembled slightly, before continuing: 'just before he died . . .'

Mitch touched Jason sympathetically on the arm.

'Your brother died?' This was news to him. 'I'm really sorry, Jason. I guess you must miss him a lot, huh?'

Jason nodded, and began to collect his baseball cards together.

'He was my best friend, Mitch. He took care of me,' he said evenly. 'Now I've learned how to take care of myself.'

Mitch looked fondly at the young boy. Jason had guts, that was for sure.

'I'm never gonna walk again, Mitch,' he continued, in a matter-of-fact way that made it clear that he had already learnt to accept the inevitable.

'Are your doctors sure about that?' Mitch queried.

Jason nodded stoically. 'I only have two chances – slim and none,' he said. 'And slim just left town.' He paused before adding: 'You're so lucky, Mitch?'

Mitch looked curiously at him. 'I'm lucky? Why's that?'

'At least you have a chance to walk again,' Jason said and sighed. 'Man, what I wouldn't give to have that chance again.' He gazed wistfully in the distance, at the basketball court where patients were speeding around in their wheelchairs. He turned back to Mitch.

'Mitch, the way you got hurt, saving that girl. If you had the chance to do it over again would you do it, even knowing what was gonna happen?'

Mitch whistled. That was a heavy subject for an eleven-year-old to be discussing with him. But then Jason was like no other eleven-year-old he had ever met before: he'd had to do a lot of growing up in a really short time.

'Jason, that is one heck of a question,' he said and thought about it. *To save that girl's life, even though he knew that it meant that he might never walk again* . . .

Finally he said: 'Yeah, I would do the same thing again. How about you?'

'I had to try to save my brother,' Jason stated firmly. 'I'd do that over and over again a million times.'

He looked around nervously, as if to make sure that nobody was watching them or listening in to their conversation.

'Mitch, if there's something I'm not supposed to tell anyone, is it OK if I tell you?'

Mitch pretended to consider the matter. 'Well, pal, that depends on if you think you can trust me or not.'

'I'm a pretty good judge of character,' Jason said airily, with all the self-assurance of a streetwise kid from downtown Chicago, and then lowered his voice. 'I'm hidin' out here till the guys who wasted my brother get on trial.' He puffed himself up with pride. 'I am gonna be the star witness!'

'Your secret is safe with me,' Mitch said solemnly and then chuckled. It was obvious that he didn't really believe Jason's story, dismissing it as just a childish fantasy. He changed the subject.

'You wanna drag race?'

'You're on!' whooped Jason, and the two of them began to race each other's wheelchairs across the lawn.

If either of them had looked across the lawn they would have seen a car pull into the adjacent car park. It was an unassuming convertible, because the driver didn't want to draw attention to himself; he had hired it this morning at LA's International Airport under a false name and using a forged set of documents.

The coldly handsome man in the driver's seat smiled evilly to himself. The crooked Detective

Ruddick had tracked down Jason; that had been the hardest part of his task.

Now came the easy part. And this was the part he really liked. The easy part was going to be killing him.

# Chapter Six

The following morning Sophie leant against the side of the van and felt the warm sun on her face. She'd taken the day off and was determined that she was going to have the best time of her life in the company of some of her favourite people.

Mitch and Jason came careering up to her, riding their wheelchairs like they thought they were racing cars. Following them closely behind, on roller skates, was Hobie, who had been introduced to Jason by his dad and was now getting on well with the kid from Chicago.

Jason skidded to a halt in front of Sophie. 'Hobie said you had a surprise for me.'

Sophie smiled. 'Actually it's a surprise for you *and* Mitch,' she said.

Mitch was just as much in the dark as Jason.

Sophie glanced over at Hobie as if to say: *Well, honey, shall we let them in on our li'l secret and tell them?*

Hobie nodded.

'What's going on,' said Sophie, 'is that *I* am going to the beach!'

'The beach?' gasped Jason 'Wow, are you ever lucky! I've only seen pictures of the beach.'

'Well, how'd you like to go there for real?' Hobie asked his new friend.

'Get outta here!'

'Nope!' said Sophie, and pulled down the ramp which led up into the van. 'Get in there, both of you!' she said with the authority of someone who is absolutely determined that all her friends were going to have the time of their lives whether they liked it or not. 'We're all heading to the beach!'

Hobie pushed Jason and his wheelchair into the van, but Mitch hung back. Sophie looked knowingly at him.

'Are you coming, Mitch?' she asked, in a tone of voice which would brook no disagreement.

'I . . . uh, I don't know,' he said.

Sophie understood instantly what the problem was; it was partly because of this that she had arranged this outing with Hobie and kept it secret from Mitch.

Mitch was *scared*, she realised, scared of

going back to Baywatch, scared of returning a
cripple to the place where he lived and worked
as an able-bodied lifeguard. Scared of what his
friends would think.

*Well, he's gonna have to go back there some
day, either on two legs or two wheels, so it might
as well be now!* she decided, and, before Mitch
could protest, pushed him up the ramp and into
the van. *And we are all going to have a good
time even if it kills us!*

As the van pulled away from the car lot, so
Ruddick's hired car slipped out, following them
at a discreet distance. By tonight Jason was
going to be dead, Ruddick determined; he was
going to be several tens of thousands of bucks
richer; and his drugs-baron boss was going to
be in the clear.

*

Jason could hardly believe the magnificent
sight before him: the Pacific Ocean, glittering
in the early-afternoon sun, and a deeper blue
than he had ever imagined in his wildest
dreams.

The contrast between this and the inner-city
slums of Chicago left him, for the first time in
his short life, simply lost for words. This was
better than he had ever imagined; heck, it

was even better than a grandstand seat at the baseball World Series!

'Sophie, can I take Jason for a tour of the bike path?' Hobie asked.

Sophie seemed unsure. She knew what the two kids were planning on doing: seeing which of them could beat the other in a race.

'Hey, it's real safe,' said Hobie. 'It's off the main road. And I'll be really careful – I'll stay right on the bike path.'

Jason looked up hopefully at Sophie, with big melting brown eyes.

'OK,' she sighed, bowing to the inevitable. 'But don't you speed demons go knocking anyone off the path, you hear!'

With a whoop of joy the two boys sped off, Jason in his wheelchair, Hobie on his roller skates. Sophie turned back and walked over to Mitch who was looking towards the beach with yearning in his eyes.

Down on the beach a group of blonde-haired German tourists were having a game of volley-ball, while in the distance a father and his son were throwing a frisbee to each other. Along the shoreline a pair of joggers were taking an early-afternoon run, and in the water itself a speedboat was pulling two water skiers through the ocean. Up in the sky a hang-glider sailed and soared in the thermals.

*And I'm stuck here in this blasted wheelchair!*
Mitch cursed. *Hell, I can't even get up and feel
the sand between my toes!*

Sophie came up to him. 'You OK, sugar?' she
asked.

Mitch looked over at the lookout tower down
on the beach. It seemed years since he had
stood on that tower, keeping watch on the beach
and the ocean. It had, in fact, been only a week.

'I think I'm gonna go down and say hi to
Matt,' he said.

'Sure, if you want to be alone,' she said. 'I
understand . . .'

'Thanks,' said Mitch, and meant it. He began
to wheel himself down to the beach.

When he reached the tower he found Matt
staring out to sea. The young Mediterranean-
looking hunky lifeguard was a good friend of
Mitch; Matt had a lot of the qualities Mitch had
had at his age.

Mitch called out to him and Matt turned and
raced down the steps from the look-out plat-
form, taking them two at a time.

*The steps I can't climb any longer,* Mitch
thought ruefully.

'Mitch!' cried Matt, and gave his friend a welcoming slap on the back. He looked Mitch
straight in the eyes, purposely avoiding looking

at his wheelchair. 'How's it goin', man? We missed you.'

'I miss you all too,' he admitted, and then sighed with pleasure. 'God, it's great being back at the beach, you know. I forgot how beautiful it is. I forgot what it was like being a lifeguard . . .'

Matt frowned. '*Was*? You make it sound as though you're not coming back . . .'

'Haven't you heard?' Mitch said bitterly. 'I'm not coming back.' He turned the wheelchair around. 'Anyway, great seeing you, man . . . I – I gotta go check on Hobie.'

For a second Matt stood there, not quite believing what he was hearing. *This isn't the Mitch I know*, he thought. *The Mitch who pushed me through rookie school and made sure that I came out Rookie of the Year*!

Then he marched after Mitch, and grabbed hold of his wheelchair, forcing him to stop.

'Mitch, I'm not gonna let you do this to yourself,' he said firmly.

'Do what?'

'Give up!' Matt practically spat out the words. 'You told me when I was at rookie school that I was a quitter! Well, I was. But you went and told me to fight for what I believed in!'

'I am fighting!' Mitch snapped back, losing his temper with both himself and Matt. 'I just don't know what the hell I'm fighting for!'

Matt was about to say something when there was a cry from the fast-food stand and open-air bar up the boardwalk overlooking the beach. There was the crash of breaking glass as two men, a Chinese and an Italian, launched into a drunken fight. Tables were overturned and there were screams of panic from the others in the bar as the two drunks threw themselves against each other.

Matt looked at Mitch. There were still things they had to discuss. 'I'll be right back, OK,' he said.

Matt raced across the beach on powerful legs, and reached the bar in seconds. He leapt on to the Italian who was battering away at the Chinese, and pulled him off. The Chinese guy, however, seemed to see this as just an opportunity to kick the Italian in the stomach and the force of the blow threw both Matt and the Italian to the floor.

Matt jumped instantly to his feet, as the Chinese, out of his head on cheap alcohol, launched into him. He struck at Matt, who parried his blow and followed it with one of his own. The Chinese staggered back, falling unconscious to the floor, and Matt turned to the Italian. Now that his opponent had been put temporarily out of action he decided that Matt would make an easy target. But Matt was far

more clear-headed than the drunk and skilfully
stepped out of his way and came up behind
him, locking him in a firm half-Nelson.

From the beach Mitch watched, as a police
patrol car came up and Matt handed the two
drunks over to them. He had known that the
drunks would be no match for Matt and that
he wasn't in any danger. In fact, the small
fracas had even been fun to watch in a strange
way. But Matt's agility and handling of the two
trouble makers had just reminded Mitch even
more painfully of his own incapacity.

As Mitch sat watching the police take the two
punks away and Matt being congratulated by
the other drinkers and thanked by the bar man-
ager, he heard a scream behind him. He spun
his wheelchair around.

About fifty metres down the beach a young
girl was thrashing about in the water near the
end of the broken-down old jetty. She was obviously in some trouble and she was panicking.
She probably had cramp or had been stung by
a jellyfish, Mitch supposed. The waters were
shallow down by the jetty at this time of day,
but Mitch knew that you can drown in only a
few inches of water.

Instinctively, he tried to rise to his feet and,
when he couldn't, almost toppled over before
throwing himself back down angrily into the

seat of his wheelchair. He screamed out to Matt, who came racing over the sands and into the water, swimming out to the girl.

Mitch turned away. Matt was a good lifeguard, one of the very best, and he knew that the girl was safe in his hands.

And he, too, used to be one of the very best lifeguards, until . . . He looked down resentfully at his two useless, unmoving legs, and punched them angrily with his fists, as if to pound some feeling or life back into them.

Mitch Buchannon, once the top lifeguard at Baywatch, with so many trophies he didn't know what to do with them all, felt like an old, old man, frustrated, useless and totally ineffectual.

Devastated, he wheeled himself back up to the boardwalk.

*

'Man, can't you go a little faster than this?' Jason complained good-naturedly. 'You're goin' real slow!'

Roller-skated Hobie was pushing Jason's wheelchair as fast as he could, down the bike path which ran the whole length of the promenade. Running parallel to the path was the main road, down which cars whizzed on their way to the other beaches of the South Californian coast. From a distance, one particular car was keeping close tabs on the two boys.

Jason was loving it all: the salt-smell of the ocean, the brightness of the Californian sun as it was reflected off the water and the golden beach, and the Californian bathing beauties lying out on the sand, paying some serious attention to their tans. He remembered the reeking and graffiti-covered walls of the ten-ement blocks back in Chicago, the noise of police sirens wailing way into the night, and the junkies and good-time girls on every street corner. *Hey*! he said to himself. *There just ain't no competition*!

'Boy, the beach is the greatest!' he said to Hobie. 'I just love being here!'

'You'd love the water too,' said Hobie, who had been able to swim long before he'd learnt to walk. 'I could help you learn how to swim.'

'My brother tried to teach me once,' admitted Jason. 'I just couldn't do it.' And then with typi-cal candour he added: 'I was just too scared.'

Hobie laughed. 'Well, I wouldn't want you to be scared – except by a daredevil speed skater!'

And with a mighty shove, Hobie pushed his friend's wheelchair hard, increasing his speed as they sped down the bicycle path, trying to outrace the cars on the road.

Suddenly there was a screech of tyres and the car which had been following them drove off the road, trying to cut straight across their path. In the millisecond before it turned towards them, Hobie spotted it out of the corner of his eye.

With a yelp of panic, he threw both himself and Jason off the bicycle path and on to the grass verge, from which they tumbled down to the beach. The car ripped back on to the road and sped off into the distance.

Hobie crawled over to Jason who was lying dazed by his overturned wheelchair. 'You OK, Jason?' he asked, full of concern.

Jason pulled himself into a sitting position and stared angrily after the quickly vanishing car.

'That guy musta been crazy!' he growled.

'Or drunk,' agreed Hobie.

He clambered to his feet and began to climb back up the grass verge. 'C'mon, we gotta get back,' he said, until a call from Jason made him turn round.

Jason was still lying on the ground beside his wheelchair. In the heat of the moment Hobie had forgotten that his friend couldn't walk.

'Any time of day will be fine for you to help me up!' Jason said sarcastically as Hobie rushed down to help him back into the wheelchair.

'Sorry,' said Hobie. It was just that Jason acted so, well, so normal; it was difficult to realise that he was disabled in any way.

'And Jason, you gotta promise not to tell my dad a word of what's just happened. If he gets to hear about it he'll never let us near the beach again.'

Jason nodded. 'OK, I promise.'

Unknown to the young boy it was a promise that could mean his death.

# Chapter Seven

Detective Ruddick waited in a deserted clearing off the main road, some fifty miles from the coast. He'd been waiting for over half an hour now, but then his boss liked to keep people waiting. It made them nervous and edgy, and easier to manipulate.

Finally, a long black cadillac with tinted windows scrunched to a halt in a lay-by, and the driver – a great hulk of a man dressed in an austere black uniform – got out and opened the passenger door.

A small, slight, elderly man, dressed smartly in an Armani suit and with his silver-white hair perfectly coiffured, got out and breathed in the fresh country air. He looked like any successful businessman going out for a late-afternoon stroll; the only difference was that

the business he dealt in was not stocks and
bonds but heroin and cocaine.

After a while, he affected to notice the waiting detective and walked slowly towards him.
His chauffeur followed at a discreet distance.

'Hello, Mr Ruddick,' said the elderly man,
and smiled. It was the smile of the crocodile
approaching its next meal. He put a friendly
arm over Ruddick's shoulder and they walked
further on into the clearing.

'Tell me, Frankie, how long have I known
you?' he asked. 'Since you were in high school?'

'No, Mr Macieri,' said Ruddick, remembering
the day when he was a impecunious student,
and the drugs baron had befriended him. 'It
was my freshman year in college.'

'I picked you myself,' said Macieri. 'I opened
the door for you . . .'

It was true. Macieri had helped him through
college when his parents couldn't afford to; and,
when Ruddick had graduated, he had even
recommended him to the Chief of Police, who,
he claimed, was a personal friend of his. And
since that day he had never let Ruddick forget
it.

In return Ruddick performed several
'services' for him, vital services that ensured
that in over fifteen years of breaking the law

Macieri had kept a reputation unblemished by
any hint of corruption or criminality.

'I'll get rid of the kid, don't worry,' Ruddick
assured his boss.

'But I *am* worried,' said Macieri in a soft voice
which nevertheless carried the promise of real
menace. 'Here we are just a week away from
the trial. They could put our Chicago operation
out of business. And you blow a simple attempt
to get rid of a kid in a wheelchair!'

'It's tough to get him alone!' protested Ruddick. 'He's always hanging out with this crippled lifeguard!'

'Well, if this lifeguard becomes a problem,
then you must get rid of him too,' he replied
calmly, as if he were discussing a simple business transaction.

He regarded Ruddick through steely, serpen-
tine eyes. 'I *own* you, Frankie,' he said. 'I made
you what you are and I put you where you are.
But if this kid lives to testify I put you in the
ground!' He smiled at his employee. 'Got it?'

And with that the drugs baron left the trem-
bling detective. Ruddick walked slowly back to
his own hired car, and felt the gun in the con-
cealed shoulder holster underneath his
designer jacket.

*What Mr Macieri wants Mr Macieri gets*, he
realised. *And, if this Buchannon guy gets in my*

*way, then he gets blasted away along with the kid!*

# Chapter Eight

Mitch lay in his bed staring up at the ceiling.
It had been another gruelling morning with
Sophie putting him through his paces once
again in the gym and then in the therapy pool,
where he felt such a fool having to be put into
the overhead chair and then lowered in the
water with a pulley. He was exhausted and was
taking a well-deserved rest before lunch.

As he turned over in his bed, he saw his
empty wheelchair standing there waiting for
him. It had become a part of him, the first thing
he saw when he woke up in the morning and
the last thing he saw when he went to sleep at
night. It had become as familiar to him as the
slippers he left under his bed at home, or
the dressing gown he always hung on the back
of his bedroom door.

And he hated it.

He closed his eyes and remembered a friend of his from way back when he was still a rookie lifeguard. Turner had been a lifeguard but one day he did a badly-judged dive and ended up shattering his spine. Mitch could still remember the day he'd gone to visit his pal in hospital.

'How ya feelin'?' Mitch had asked cheerfully.

'Like racing,' Turner had answered. 'But the doc says I won't be able to do it for a while . . . well, the word he used was "never" actually . . .' Turner had grinned at him. 'But he doesn't know the heart of a lifeguard like we do, does he, Mitch!'

'No, too damn right he doesn't.'

'Right. And you'd better keep on workin' out, 'cause I'm gonna be out of here soon and I'm gonna beat ya!'

'There's a whole bunch of people waiting downstairs, all dying to see you,' Mitch had said. 'Are you up to that – I mean, can I bring them up?'

'Yeah..'

And then Turner had turned to Mitch. And there was a horribly frightened look on his face. He glanced over to his wheelchair which, like Mitch's, had become so much a part of him, a cruel cold reminder of the fact that he couldn't walk.

'*Do me a favour, Mitch,*' he had said, his voice quaking with emotion. '*Get rid of that thing for me, will ya?*'

'*It's outta here.*'

\*

Sophie's voice cut into Mitch's reverie.

'You know, Mitch, that wheelchair is not your enemy,' she said, reading his thoughts.

'I had a friend once who was paralysed,' said Mitch sadly. 'He swore that he'd walk again . . .' He laughed bitterly: Turner had never stood on his own two feet again. 'He was only fooling himself . . .'

'Honey, everybody's a fool for at least five minutes every day,' Sophie said, not unkindly. 'Wisdom comes from not exceeding the limit!'

Something inside Mitch seemed to snap. What right did Sophie have to lecture him? She wasn't the one who couldn't walk, she wasn't the one stuck in a hospital bed! She was the one who could walk, who could swim, who could dance, who could run! Who was she to tell him what to do or how to feel!

'What are you talking about!' he barked angrily. 'Why don't you just go and leave me alone!'

Sophie folded her arms and looked at Mitch

like an elementary schoolteacher reprimanding
a pupil who's just thrown a tantrum. Mitch's
harsh and angry words seemed to have had no
effect on her whatsoever.

'Honey, resisting me is like challenging a
school of piranhas to a game of water polo –
you are gonna lose out every single time!' She
chuckled ironically. ' "I've been working like a
dog in my therapy sessions, can't feel a thing
in my legs, and nothing moves on its own." '

It was a list of complaints that Sophie had
heard countless times, and it was exactly what
Mitch had been thinking. 'Mind-reading,' she
said, tapping her temple. 'A little hobby of
mine.'

Mitch was impressed but bitter as well. 'Why
don't you tell me what else I'm thinking?' he
asked reproachfully.

'You tell me – it's healthier.'

'You wanna know what I'm thinking?' Mitch
said angrily. 'I'm thinking that I'll never walk
again! You know it. And I know it!'

Sophie sat down at Mitch's bedside and held
his hand. He turned his face away.

'Mitch, that is not true,' she said, willing him
to believe her. 'It could still happen. You never
know when a toe will wiggle. It might take
days, it might take weeks, or even months. But
when it does, then you're on your way!'

Mitch turned back and looked at her through narrow, unbelieving eyes. 'Would you save that talk for the dreamers?' he said bitterly.

Now it was Sophie's turn to get angry. She stood up. 'OK, so what are you telling me now?' she demanded. 'You're telling me that you're quitting, that the great Mitch Buchannon is quitting? Is that it?'

Mitch avoided Sophie's accusing glare, and tried to keep his voice steady as he said: 'No. I am telling you that I am facing facts.'

'No, that is *not* what you're telling me, Mitch Buchannon,' countered Sophie. 'You are quitting!'

'I am facing facts!'

'*You're quitting*, Mitch!' Sophie bawled out, and then lowered her voice. 'I can help you with the injury to your spine, but I cannot do anything about your other back problem.'

Mitch looked up, intrigued. 'What other back problem?' he asked.

'That streak of yellow that's runnin' straight down the middle of yours!'

# Chapter Nine

Sophie's parting words had a strong impact on Mitch. Maybe she was right, he thought, maybe he had given up all hope, refusing to struggle against adversity. It had been so easy down on the beach, he had realised; there he could be brave and dynamic, making yet another spectacular rescue as the cute girls on vacation watched on.

It was so easy having other people – either in the ocean or on one of the lookout towers – rely on him. When it came to relying on himself, having no one to depend on but himself, then it became real difficult. He recalled Matt's word's of advice to him on the beach the previous day; *fight for what you believe in*!

Propped up on his pillow, he stared down intently at his right foot, commanding it to

move. His brow was furrowed and a tiny trickle
of sweat ran down his temple as he tried to flex
his leg muscles.

*Move, damn you, move just an inch! Move!*

He fell back on to the bed, overcome with
exhaustion. This was even more stressful than
a rescue down at the beach. And the results
were less: not a tremor, not a twitch, not even
a brief spasm of pain to indicate that there was
any spark of life left in his legs. Instead all he
could feel was an empty space below his waist:
his legs might as well have been cut off for all
the use they were to him now.

He turned towards the open door, only now
realising that Hobie had been watching him for
some time. He was carrying an empty can of
Coke in his hand, looking for a garbage can in
which to dump it.

'What're you doin', Dad?' he asked.

*What does it look as if I'm doing?* Mitch
thought, and chuckled.

'I'm trying to move my foot,' he said.

'And is it moving?' Hobie asked hopefully.

Mitch shrugged and shook his head.

'Well, are you trying as hard as you can?'
Hobie asked and walked around to the foot of
his dad's bed. 'Are you focusing?'

Mitch looked suspiciously at his son. 'Did
Sophie send you in here?' he asked warily.

Hobie was puzzled. 'What d'you mean?'

'It doesn't matter,' said Mitch. Hobie had, in fact, not seen Sophie all day. He had been at home, reading up on overcoming disabilities in books he'd borrowed from the local library.

Like Sophie, however, he was determined to do everything in his power to help his dad walk again and to get him back as soon as possible down on the beach – which was the only place where he really belonged or was happy.

'Dad, I bet if you really, really concentrated then you could move your foot,' Hobie said with conviction. He placed the empty can of Coke on the end of the bed, about an inch away from his Mitch's right foot. 'Try to knock this can over,' he said. 'Come on, try!'

Mitch looked at his son: there was a fierce determination in Hobie's eyes which, he realised, wouldn't stand for any opposition or negativity. Giving in to the inevitable, Mitch raised himself up on his pillow once more and gazed intently down at the Coke can and his foot.

'Focus, Dad, focus!' urged Hobie, also staring down at Mitch's foot and the can, joining his will to his dad's, visualising the power running down into Mitch's legs, imagining Mitch's foot twitching and knocking the Coke can on to the floor.

Mitch screwed up his eyes, trying to raise the power needed to move his foot. Beads of cold sweat appeared on his brow, and he could feel his heart thumping away, as he summoned up every ounce of strength in his body.

'Come on, Dad, you can do it!'

Hobie's voice rang in his ears. He was clutching his dad's arm now, so tightly that his nails dug into the flesh. But Mitch didn't feel the pain: the two most important things in the world right now were his right foot and the Coke can.

*Just an inch, just move it an inch, just an inch . . .*

He shut his eyes, concentrating on a picture of the Coke can tumbling off the side of the bed, imagining the clattering of the can as it hit the ground.

His breath was coming in gasps now, as he directed all his energies to his foot. But there was no response, no response at all.

*It's no use*, thought Mitch, *it's never going to move!*

'You can do it, Dad!' shouted Hobie. 'Just try a little harder!'

*Come on! Just one inch! Do it for Hobie!*

'Try! Try harder!'

*It's no blasted good! I can't do it! I can't even do it for my own son!*

Mitch suddenly pushed himself up off his pillow and swiped angrily at the Coke can with his hand. It fell clattering to the floor.

'Just leave me alone, will you!' he exploded, turning savagely towards his son.

Hobie's face fell.

'Leave me alone!'

Hobie turned and ran out of the room, his eyes streaming with tears.

A few seconds later Stephanie, who had just arrived at the Rehab Centre, entered the room. There was an angry look on her face as she regarded Mitch, who had sunk back into his pillow and was looking away from the door through which Hobie had fled.

'Your son just ran out of the room crying,' she said icily. Mitch turned to look at her. His face was sad and despondent: he was already regretting his sudden outburst.

'I know, I know,' he said, guiltily. 'I got frustrated and I took it out on him.'

'You're an adult, Mitch, and Hobie's only a child,' Stephanie said accusingly; 'And he's scared to death.'

'Well, adults can be scared to death too!' Mitch countered angrily.

Stephanie moved over to Mitch's bedside and laid a comforting sympathetic hand on his.

'Look, I know this is hard for you now, Mitch,'

she said, and her voice was no longer harsh
and disapproving. 'But Hobie needs you . . .'

Mitch hung his head: Stephanie was right, he
realised that. And Hobie was more important to
him than his stupid pride or self-esteem. Hell,
even if he lost the power to walk forever, there
was no way he was going to lose Hobie.

'I know,' he said finally, his voice full of con-
trition. 'I'm sorry.'

'It's not me you should apologise to, Mitch,'
Stephanie said softly.

Mitch nodded. 'I'll go find him,' he said. Stephanie began to help him out of his bed and
into his wheelchair.

*

Hobie sat on a bench disconsolately, sobbing.
A little way off a group of wheelchair-bound
patients were playing a game of basketball.
Why couldn't his dad be like them? he asked
himself. They weren't sitting around – well, in
wheelchairs maybe they were – they weren't
sitting around feeling sorry for themselves.
They were making the most of their circum-
stances, getting on with their lives as best as
they could. Why couldn't his dad? His dad had
helped thousands of people down at Baywatch
why couldn't he now let others help him?

Hobie was aware of someone beside him. He
quickly dried his eyes and glanced over to see
Jason who was looking at him in concern. As
always the young lad was carrying his pack of
baseball cards in his lap.

'Hobie, what's wrong?'

'Nothin',' Hobie lied. 'I'm fine.'

Jason fixed his friend with a seen-it-all-and-
you-ain't-gonna-pull-the-wool-over-my-eyes
sort of stare.

'I'm in a wheelchair, man,' he pointed out. 'I
ain't in no coma! Now, come on, what's goin'
on?'

'Nothing,' Hobie insisted and then looked
searchingly at the young black lad. 'Wh-what's
it's like, Jason? I mean, *really* like?'

'What's what like?'

Hobie felt awkward but finally brought himself to say the dreaded word: 'You know – being
paralysed . . .'

Jason sat back in his wheelchair and thought.
'That's a kinda hard question,' he began. 'But
it's like every day when I wake up, for the tin-
iest second I forget that I have to get help to get
out of bed and into the wheelchair.' He sighed
bitterly. 'And then the whole rest of my day,
man, there's no way that I can ever forget . . .'

'Do you ever get mad?' Hobie asked.

'Sure I do! Sometimes I get mad because that

tiny second in the morning just can't last all day . . .'

Hobie stared down at his feet as he continued self-consciously: 'Do you ever get mad at someone you love?'

Jason nodded wisely to himself: everything had just fallen into place. 'Your dad got mad at you, didn't he?'

Hobie nodded.

'I used to get mad at my mom,' Jason continued. 'But she knew that it didn't mean that I didn't love her or anything like that. It's easy to get mad at someone who loves you because you know they'll always forgive you.' He glanced over to the far end of the lawn: Mitch and Stephanie had come out of the main building and were watching them.

'Look, Hobie, I gotta go now,' he said. 'Sophie will kill me if I'm late for therapy again.'

'Bye, Jason,' Hobie said as his friend wheeled himself away. 'And thanks . . .'

As Jason departed, Mitch left Stephanie and pushed himself slowly over to the bench on which Hobie was sitting. He felt awkward and avoided his son's eyes as he began:

'Look, uh . . . Hey . . . Well, what I mean to say is . . .' He looked up into Hobie's expectant face. 'I'm sorry that I lost it with you just now,' he said finally. 'It's just that I'm having a really

hard time with this and I'm tryin' really hard
to beat it. Sometimes I just get a little
frustrated . . .' He smiled hopefully at his son.

'Forgive me?' he asked.

Hobie leant over and put his arms around
his dad; there were tears in his eyes once more,
but this time they were tears of joy.

'I forgive you, Dad.'

Mitch stifled a sob himself. 'You know that I
love you, don't you, Hobie?'

'I love you too,' Hobie confirmed, as Mitch
drew his son even more tightly to him.

Suddenly both of them became aware of the
shouts and cries of the basketball players on
the nearby court. Mitch released Hobie from
his embrace, and glanced over to the players.
They were all having a great time and, for
people confined to wheelchairs, they were doing
a real good job passing the ball around and
hurling it up into the net. Heck, it even looked
like *fun!*

Mitch looked down at his own wheelchair and
there was a mischievous twinkle in his eyes.

'Hobie, what do you say that we go teach
those guys how to play that game?'

Hobie's face lit up. 'All riiiiight!'

Hobie ran over to the basketball game, followed by Mitch in his wheelchair. From the
distance Stephanie watched Mitch and Hobie

enter the game; this was what Mitch needed, she realised, something to take his mind off his troubles, something to make him realise that life goes on whether you're in a wheelchair or not.

A sudden wave of despair crashed over her and she hugged herself for comfort. She remembered what the doctor had told her when they had first brought Mitch in: *The odds for a full recovery are about five per cent.*

*Five per cent.*

*Please, please, let him walk again. Please let him find the will to walk again!*

# Chapter Ten

*You only miss someone when they're gone*, Stephanie realised as she filed her reports in the main operations room at Baywatch headquarters. Everyone was used to Mitch's presence in headquarters or down on the beach or in his lookout tower. He was so much a part of the scene at Baywatch that they hardly ever noticed him – well, insofar as one can hardly notice a tall, hunky lifeguard with a wicked sense of humour and twinkling, mischievous eyes.

But now that he was no longer here the days seemed to drag, the operations room seemed quieter and emptier, and her work at Baywatch seemed more of a chore than it had ever done before. She sighed and massaged her temples: the stress of doing Mitch's job as well as her own, looking after Hobie, and worrying about Mitch was beginning to tell on her. What she really needed, she realised, was a vacation and then smiled wryly as she remembered how her last vacation, on board a cruise liner with Mitch, had turned out.

She looked up as Matt and Summer came in. Matt with his hunky good looks, and the blonde-haired elfin Summer made a good pair, even though each of them was seeing someone else. Matt was seeing CJ, another lifeguard and an old friend of Mitch and Stephanie, while Summer was going out with Jimmy Slade, the champion surfer, who everybody was saying ought to turn professional.

'Hi, guys,' Stephanie said, and then saw just how tired the two looked. 'Hard day?'

Matt threw himself down on to a chair. 'It seems like no one knew how to swim today,' he complained. 'I spent more time in the water than I did in my tower!'

'That's the job, Matt,' smiled Stephanie.

'Stephanie . . .' Summer began hesitantly. 'Uh . . . Matt and I were wondering if we could switch towers tomorrow . . .'

Stephanie frowned. 'Switch towers? Whatever for?'

Summer looked over to Matt for help: if Ste-

phanie found out the real reason why she
wanted to swap with Matt . . .

Matt stood up. 'I just wanted to get more
experience in a different tower,' he lied. It was
a pretty flimsy excuse and he knew it. He just
hoped that Stephanie would buy it for Summer's sake.

'It sounds like you're getting a lot of experience right where you are, Matt,' Stephanie said
as she studied the list of tower assignments for
the following day.

Summer was about to say something when
the door burst open and CJ stepped in. 'Hi,
guys!' she said brightly. 'What's up?'

Stephanie looked suspiciously at Matt and
Summer, making them feel like two errant
school kids being brought up in front of the
headmistress.

'I haven't quite figured that out yet,' Stephanie said.

CJ shrugged, and turned to Matt. 'Say, wasn't
that Jimmy I saw surfing in front of your tower
today?' she asked her boyfriend.

*Shoot!* thought Summer.

Matt cast a sideways glance at Summer. 'I
think so . . .'

The penny had dropped for Stephanie; she
realised why Matt had agreed to swap towers

with Summer tomorrow. She got up angrily from her desk and walked to Matt.

'You *think* so?' she asked icily. 'A great surfer like Jimmy Slade either is or is not surfing in front of your tower, Matt. There's no mistaking it.' She turned on Summer. 'What is a mistake though, Summer, is to try and get a tower near your boyfriend!'

Summer shifted awkwardly under Stephanie's disapproving gaze. 'Well, that's not exactly what I was doing . . .' she said weakly.

'Isn't it?'

'No, not exactly . . .' Summer's voice tailed off: she'd been found out and she knew it. Stephanie, who always played strictly by the rules, would never let her swap towers now.

'I'm surprised at you, Summer,' she said. 'This is totally unprofessional. If Mitch were here, he'd – '

And then she realised that Mitch wasn't here, and the fear that he might never return crashed down on her. She spun on her heel and marched into Mitch's small office, slamming the door behind her.

A few minutes later there was a tentative knock at the door, and Summer came in, followed by Matt and CJ. Stephanie looked up from the desk: her eyes were pink and she'd been trying to stop herself from sobbing. On top of the desk there was a photo of Mitch and Hobie, taken at DisneyWorld; Mitch was standing holding the young Hobie in his arms. *Standing* . . .

Summer went up to the desk. 'Stephanie, I'm really sorry,' she apologised. 'I feel really stupid even thinking about getting to be near Jimmy when Mitch may not even . . .' She dried up as she couldn't find the words to express what she was feeling.

'What Summer's trying to say is that we all miss him too,' said Matt.

'Yeah,' said CJ, who had known Mitch much longer than Matt or Summer. She walked around the office, running her fingers along some of Mitch's swimming trophies which he'd hung on the office walls when he'd run out of space at home. 'Nothing's the same here without Mitch . . .' She chuckled, and then burst out laughing.

'What's so funny?' asked Stephanie.

'Remember that big rescue Mitch went out on before rookie school started?' she asked. 'And when he called us all in for back-up . . .'

The four of them cast their minds back to that time, months ago now, when Mitch had spotted something floating in the water. There had been a number of tourists in difficulties in the water recently and the Pacific had seemed to have been more troublesome and deadly than usual. There had also been reports of sharks in the water. Mitch was taking no chances and had called a red alert, calling in all available units.

The rookie lifeguards had also been called into the operation and Matt and Summer had joined in the rescue mission, while Stephanie and CJ piloted the yellow scarab to the scene of the action.

Mitch had been first in the water, swimming furiously out to the body in the water. He prayed that he would be in time: a few seconds could mean the difference between life and death for a victim in the water.

With a final powerful thrust of his legs he reached the victim, at the same time as the scarab and Matt and Summer did. If he'd been on dry land Mitch would have wished for the ground beneath him to open up and swallow him. As it was he could only hide his head beneath the water in shame, as the others burst into helpless fits of laughter around him.

The 'victim' Mitch had spotted in the water and for whom he had brought into action all of Baywatch's best, had turned out to be nothing more than a brown paper bag which had been discarded by a tourist and had floated out to sea!

'You girls missed out on what we did to him in the locker room later,' Matt said, and grinned as he recalled Mitch stepping into the showers to be confronted by male lifeguards, stark naked apart from the paper bag each one had put over his head.

Matt laughed at the memory and even Stephanie was roused from her depression and joined in.

'You know, Mitch really believed in me,' said Matt, suddenly serious as he remembered his first days at Baywatch, when he didn't think he would ever make the grade as a lifeguard. With Mitch's encouragement he had ended up as Rookie of the Year. 'Without Mitch I don't think I'd be a lifeguard right now.'

CJ agreed. She'd left Baywatch to work on the American River up in gold-mining country as a guide. 'If it weren't for him I'd still be guiding rafts downriver,' she admitted. 'Thank God Mitch talked me into coming back to Baywatch!'

Summer sighed. 'I just wish there was something we could do for him,' she said. 'He's done so much for us.'

'There is something we can all do for him,' stated Stephanie. 'We can all believe that he's going to come back just the way he was.' She looked at them all, and there was a determined

gleam in her eyes, as much for her benefit as
for theirs.

'He has to come back.'

*And please God make it soon!*

# Chapter Eleven

Later that night Hobie sat at home in front of the fire, sadly watching the flames leap and twist in the old-fashioned fireplace. The smell of sweetly burning wood filled the living room.

As Hobie stared into the crackling fire he seemed to see faces in the flames, the faces of himself and Mitch. Memories came flooding back, memories which he thought he had forgotten for ever, memories of the good times he and his dad had had on the beach.

He remembered them racing each other along the shoreline, playing beach ball with Matt and Summer and the other lifeguards at Baywatch; he remembered his dad and Jimmy Slade helping him improve his surfing technique; he remembered one particular moment down at Baywatch when Mitch was lying in the sand, with his legs pointing up at the sky, balancing the giggling and outrageously happy Hobie on them.

*On his legs ...*

Stephanie touched him on the shoulder. 'Hobie?'

Hobie quickly dried his eyes. 'That fire sure makes my eyes water,' he said, embarrassed.

Stephanie smiled. 'It's OK to cry, Hobie.'

'I'm not crying,' he said and started to cry again.

'Your dad's going to be OK,' she reassured him. 'It's just going to take a little time, that's all ...'

'The doctor said he'd never walk again,' Hobie stated flatly.

'Hobie, that's not true ...'

'Oh yes it is,' he said. 'I heard you talking to the doctor in the hall when Dad had his tests. He said he only had about five chances out of a hundred.'

*Shoot!* thought Stephanie. She hadn't realised that Hobie had been eavesdropping on their conversation. She reached over and hugged Hobie. There were tears in Stephanie's eyes now.

'When have you known your dad never to beat the odds?' she asked. 'I know you're scared,

Hobie, and I'm scared too . . . But we have to be strong for your dad . . .'

Hobie nodded. 'I want to,' he sobbed. 'But I don't know if I can . . .'

Stephanie forced Hobie to look into her eyes. 'Well, I know you can,' she declared. 'Your dad started rehab today, and it's going to be tough. He's going to need you, Hobie. He's going to need you like he's never needed you before!'

*

The following day Sophie had really put Mitch through his paces and he had begun to respond to her treatment. There was still no feeling in his legs, but he had started to look at things much more positively. Sophie had expressed her approval and, as an extra treat, had allowed Hobie, Stephanie and Ben to stay after the normal visiting hours had finished. The four of them were sitting around a table playing a game of cards.

Hobie let out a cheer as he presented yet another winning hand to the others. Mitch chuckled: Hobie sure was on a winning streak tonight, he thought. If they had been playing for money, and not matchsticks, he would have won a small fortune by now.

The door opened and Sophie walked in, a finger to her lips, urging them to be quiet.

'Sorry, gang,' she whispered, 'But visiting hours have been over for nearly fifty minutes now. I cannot stretch it any longer.'

Hobie rushed over to Sophie's side and tugged at her sleeve. 'Aw, c'mon, Sophie, just one more game!' he pleaded with her, looking up imploringly with his big brown eyes. 'We'll be quiet!'

'No!' Sophie said firmly.

At the table Ben began to gather up the playing cards. 'Sophie's right, Hobie,' he said. 'Your dad needs the rest so that Sophie can punish him again tomorrow.'

Sophie looked evilly at Mitch. 'If he can take it,' she said ominously.

'I can take anything you can dish out!' Mitch said defiantly.

Sophie raised an interested eyebrow, as though Mitch had just issued her with a new challenge, a challenge which Mitch would probably live to regret.

'Good . . . I'm going to get Jason from the therapy room. Goodnight . . .'

'Tell him I'll pop by and see him,' Mitch said as she left the room.

'OK, guys,' said Stephanie. 'Tomorrow is a new game!' She took Mitch's wheelchair and

began to push him towards the elevator. Ben
and a reluctant Hobie followed.

                    *

Down in the reception area on the ground floor
Emily, the pretty young nurse on night duty,
was admiring the new doctor. She hadn't seen
him around before, which was a pity because
he was something of a hunk. A firm square
jaw, brilliantly blue eyes, and beneath his white
coat, she imagined, a body to die for.

He flashed her a dazzling white smile as she
handed him the file he had requested. He flip-
ped cursorily through it.

'Jason Saunders' room is two-twelve, Doctor,'
she said, wondering what the chances were of
the dishy doc ever giving her a date.

'Thank you, Nurse,' the doctor said crisply,
and handed her back the file. 'I appreciate your
help.'

He turned and headed for the elevator whose
doors were just opening to let out Mitch and
the others. As Stephanie wheeled Mitch out she
too caught sight of the handsome new doctor.

She looked him up and down approvingly,
from the top of his classically handsome face to
his trendy Gucci shoes. She thought briefly how

unusual it was for a doctor to be wearing designer loafers.

'Hi,' she breathed, and stopped the wheelchair to look up into his ice-blue eyes.

The doctor smiled: the attraction was obviously mutual. 'Hi.'

'Are you a new doctor here?' she asked. Like Emily, Stephanie hadn't seen him around the Rehab Centre before.

'No, I'm a visiting doctor,' he said. 'I'm here to see a patient . . .'

'Come on, Stephanie!' cried Hobie who was waiting by the exit doors.

Stephanie shrugged, and with a flirtatious wave at the handsome doctor wheeled Mitch on.

In the elevator Ruddick breathed a sigh of relief. That had been a close call. As the elevator doors slid shut he reached automatically inside the doctor's white coat he had stolen: his gun was still there in its shoulder holster. He smiled to himself.

And soon Jason would be dead.

By the exit doors Mitch was saying goodbye to his friends. Hobie looked enquiringly at his father.

'Dad, I was wondering if I could stay the night here?' he asked, and then added quickly:

'I'd be real quiet, and you wouldn't even know I was here – I promise.'

Mitch grinned and ruffled his son's hair. '*You'll* be quiet?' he said in disbelief. 'Wrong! We'll play cards again another night, OK?' He turned to Stephanie and Ben. 'And you guys, thank you very much for making sure that everything's OK at the house and with Hobie.' He looked down at his feet. 'It could be a while longer . . .'

'You just concentrate on feeling better,' Ben said cheerily. 'Because, when you do, you and I are gonna have a race with our canes!'

Mitch laughed, and waved them goodbye as they left for the car park and Ben's pick-up truck which was going to drive them all home. Mitch turned sadly away, and wheeled himself towards the reception desk. He'd promised that he'd go and see Jason before lights out, but first of all there was something else he had to do.

\*

The elevator doors swished open on the second floor; Ruddick marched smartly out and looked left and right. The corridor was deserted: it was 10.30 now and most of the residents in the Rehab Centre had gone to bed; those who were still up were probably in one of the TV lounges or unwinding in the recreation room. There was little chance that he would be spotted.

He strode down the corridor, checking the numbers on the doors: two-ten, two-eleven, two-twelve.

With a final look behind him to see that there was no one watching, Ruddick sneaked into Jason's room.

# Chapter Twelve

Sophie wheeled Jason along the corridor as the young lad continued what seemed an endless chat about his baseball cards. This one was Babe Ruth, he said, who'd made the highest number of bases in one season; that one was Dizzy Carlyle, who'd hit the longest home run ever in the history of the game. To Sophie, who didn't even understand the first rules of the USA's national sport, Jason might have been speaking Greek. Still, it was the young lad's great enthusiasm and she let him carry on.

'When did Mitch say he was coming by?' Jason asked as he searched in his pack of cards for a portrait of Joe DiMaggio, the one baseball player Sophie had heard of – and only because he'd once been married to Marilyn Monroe.

'Soon,' she said. 'So we'd best get you settled in quick, OK?'

'OK.'

'So put your cards away,' Sophie said. Jason obediently put them in the front pocket of his hooded sweatshirt. 'You can play with them again tomorrow.'

They reached Jason's room. Sophie pushed open the door and wheeled the boy in. The room was in darkness and, as Sophie flicked on the light switch, something dull and heavy struck her from behind. Suddenly everything went black and she fell, unconscious, to the floor.

\*

Emily, the night nurse on reception duty, smiled sweetly at Mitch as he pulled up to her desk. He was a good-looking man, she decided and, if the new doctor wasn't going to ask her for a date, maybe she could make a play for Mitch. Who cared if he was in a wheelchair or not? He looked as if he might be fun to be with.

'Good evening, Mr Buchannon,' she said.

'Hi, Emily. Could you do me a favour?' Emily nodded and Mitch continued: 'I know you keep some candy bars hidden back there somewhere. I want to take a couple to my friend, Jason Saunders.'

Emily rooted amongst the papers and files behind her desk for Jason's favourite sweets.

'He's a popular boy tonight,' she said.

'What d'you mean?' asked Mitch.

'A new doctor on the staff just went up to see him . . .'

A sixth sense told Mitch that something wasn't quite right. It was a sixth sense that had never let him down before at Baywatch, when he would know on just which part of the beach there was likely to be trouble.

'A new or a visiting doctor?' he asked, remembering the handsome doctor with whom Stephanie had flirted on their way out of the elevator.

*'I'm a visiting doctor, I'm here to see a patient . . .'*

And then Mitch remembered something Jason had told him some days ago . . . *I'm hiding out here until the guys who wasted my brother go on trial*. At the time he had dismissed it as a childish fantasy, but now . . . Alarm bells began to ring in Mitch's head.

'We don't permit visiting doctors here,' said Emily, unaware of Mitch's concern. 'It's the hospital rules . . .' She finally produced the candy bars from behind the desk to present them to Mitch.

But Mitch was already gone, racing furiously off towards the elevator.

\*

Mitch crashed open the door of Jason's room on the second floor and instantly took in the scene. The room was in chaos, and Jason, though 'helpless' in his wheelchair, had obviously put up a struggle.

Sophie was lying on the floor, and Mitch wheeled over to her. He leant down and shook her into consciousness.

'Sophie!' he cried urgently. 'What happened?'

Sophie sat up and rubbed the base of her neck. 'He got me from behind . . .'

'You all right?'

'Yes,' she said. 'Where's Jason? Mitch, where's Jason? He took Jason!'

'Where to?'

'I don't know!'

Mitch laid a calming hand on her shoulder. 'OK,' he commanded, taking charge of the situation. 'Call security!'

Sophie stumbled to her feet, and out into the corridor and the internal phone on the wall. In his wheelchair Mitch was already racing to the elevator.

'Where are you going?' Sophie asked.

'To find Jason!'

'But how do you know where he's been taken?' she asked.

Mitch pointed down to the ground. On the floor there was one of Jason's precious baseball cards.

Sophie shrugged. 'He must have dropped it in the struggle,' she suggested.

Mitch shook his head. *Jason drop his precious baseball cards by accident? No way!*

About ten feet away from the baseball card there was another; and at a similar distance from that, by the double doors of the elevator, there was another one.

Sophie grinned and sighed with admiration. *Well, I never . . .* she thought. *That cunning little streetwise kid!*

Jason was leaving a trail for them.

*

Gagged, and bound tightly to his wheelchair, Jason was being pushed roughly down the darkened and deserted corridors of the Rehab Centre. Pushing the wheelchair was Ruddick, still dressed in his doctor's white coat.

He hadn't said a word to Jason from the moment he had abducted him, just stared straight ahead, with a determined and maniacal look on his cruelly handsome face.

So obsessed was he that he didn't notice Jason surreptitiously letting one baseball card after another drop from his fingers on to the floor. Jason didn't know where Ruddick was taking him; all he did know was that if Mitch and Sophie didn't find him soon he was going to be very, very dead.

*

The elevator doors opened at the first floor and Mitch sped out of the lift. He looked this way and that down the darkened corridor: nothing. The floor of the corridor was clean and uncluttered. With an angry grunt Mitch pushed himself back into the elevator and furiously stabbed the button to the first floor.

He had to find Jason soon, he realised, if he had any hope of saving the boy's life.

*But what hope does a cripple have against a deadly and able-bodied gunman?* Mitch thought fearfully.

*Only a miracle can save Jason now,* he realised with a heavy heart.

*But I'll be damned if I let him come to any harm! Jason needs me! And I am not going to let him down!*

*

Jason looked up warily at his abductor and
struggled to loosen himself from his bonds. It
was no use: Ruddick had tied them much too
tightly and expertly.

The boy looked around him. Even in the darkness he recognised where they were. Ruddick
was leading him to the therapy area, where the
gym and work-out rooms were located.

And, with a sinking heart, he realised that
that was also the location of the therapy
pool . . .

Jason silently dropped another baseball card
on to the floor, as Ruddick pushed him nearer
to an almost certain death.

*

The elevator doors swished open once again,
this time on to the ground floor. It was now
half-past-eleven and the reception area was in
darkness. Even Emily was missing, probably
gone off on her coffee break and leaving the
switchboard on night service. Also missing was
any baseball card which might provide a clue
to Jason's whereabouts.

Mitch cursed under his breath and pushed
himself back into the elevator. Jason just had to

be in the basement, he reasoned; if he had misjudged and Jason and his abductor had gone *up* in the elevator, instead of *down*, then the young kid was probably already dead.

The elevator seemed to take unbearably long minutes to reach the basement, in fact it took him fewer than ten seconds. Mitch hurtled out through the open doors, and looked to his left down the shadowy corridor.

Nothing.

He jerked his head to the right.

Nothing.

*Damn it, nothing!*

And then he saw it, almost hidden in the shadows: Jason's picture card of Joe DiMaggio. Mitch picked up the card: Joltin' Joe had never been a quitter and he wasn't going to be one now.

Mitch scanned the corridor before him, searching for another card. And sure enough, a few metres from that there was another, and another, and another, all leading down to the therapy area.

He pushed on down the corridor. There was no time to lose: Jason's life was in the balance.

*

Jason's life was literally in the balance. Rud-

dick had reached the pool area where he had
roughly manhandled the young boy out of his
wheelchair and, despite Jason's kicks and muf-
fled screams of protest, had succeeded in strapping him into the overhead chair which was
normally used to lower disabled patients down
into the water. Jason's eyes widened with terror
as he realised what Ruddick's plan was.

Once Jason was firmly secured in the chair,
Ruddick went over to the poolside where he
picked up the remote control device which
would activate the overhead pulley system. He
punched the controls and the chair was hoisted
in the air and pulled slowly over, until it was
hanging directly over the centre of the pool.

Jason looked down, terrified, at the water.
Not only could he not swim but, bound and
gagged as he was, it would only take a matter
of a few minutes before he drowned.

With a cruel, sadistic laugh, Ruddick stabbed
at another button on the remote control. Pul-
leys grinding, the chair began to descend into
the pool, and Jason began to feel the water rise
up to his ankles.

And then to his knees.

And his waist.

And his neck.

He struggled wildly in his bonds. It was no
use. Ruddick had tied them too well. Jason tried

to hold his head above the level of the water but in his heart of hearts he knew that it was all going to be in vain.

Within minutes, no matter how hard he struggled to break free, he would be dead. And his brother's death would have been for nothing.

And Ruddick and his bosses would have won.

# Chapter Thirteen

Mitch hurtled at breakneck speed down the deserted corridors, praying that he wasn't going to be too late. He reached the closed doors leading to the pool area and peered through the windows.

He assessed the situation in an instant. Ruddick was standing with his back to Mitch, operating the remote control and lowering the bound and struggling Jason into the water. Mitch knew from experience that Ruddick had to keep his hands on the control all the time; if he took his fingers off for one second then the chair would stop its descent into the pool. Only this morning Sophie had been lowering Mitch into the pool and, when he'd cracked a particularly unfortunate joke, the physiotherapist had

taken her hands off the remote control and left
Mitch dangling there until he had apologised.

It was essential, therefore, that Mitch sepa-
rated Ruddick from the remote control device.
Ruddick was able-bodied and strong while
Mitch was confined to a wheelchair; the only
thing that Mitch had on his side was the
element of surprise.

*Well, it's now or never,* he decided and, with a
mighty push on the wheels of his chair, crashed
through the double doors leading to the pool.

Ruddick had hardly time to turn around
before Mitch hurtled into the crooked detective,
sending him flying, and, most importantly,
knocking the remote control from his hand.

The chair stopped its descent as the water
reached Jason's chin. He had been saved just
in the nick of time. But for how long? Ruddick
had already risen to his feet and had whipped
out his revolver from the shoulder holster
underneath his doctor's white coat. He
advanced slowly on Mitch, an evil sneer distort-
ing his handsome features, and showing him as
the sadistic pervert he really was.

*This one is gonna be real easy,* he chuckled to
himself. *Like shooting fish in a barrel. A crippled lifeguard. First him, and then the kid.*

But Ruddick had underestimated his
opponent and the skill Mitch had acquired in

racing Jason through the long winding corridors of the Rehab Centre. With another mighty spin of his wheels Mitch charged headlong into Ruddick, head-butting him in the stomach. Once again taken totally by surprise, Ruddick fell headlong into the water of the pool, dragging Mitch in after him. The gun flew from his hands, skidding along the side of the pool.

The two men sank in the waters of the pool, thrashing about and punching each other in the face and stomach. Normally Mitch would have been the stronger of the two, but with the loss of use of his legs he floundered about in the water like a novice swimmer.

The two of them rose to the surface; Ruddick slugged Mitch in the face and tried to push him under. Mitch retaliated, trying to kick his assailant in the groin, to no avail: even in the natural buoyancy of the water his legs still refused to move.

In the centre of the pool Jason struggled, trying to free himself from his bonds, and watched as Mitch and Ruddick fought to the death. Mitch wrenched Ruddick off him, and sent him flying back into the water with a terrific thump to his solar plexus.

With a snarl the crook launched himself upon Mitch again, but the lifeguard, using only his arms, managed to swim out of Ruddick's way.

He came up behind him and tried to grasp
his opponent in a half-Nelson. Ruddick kicked
Mitch viciously in the stomach, winding him,
and turned to deliver a final blow.

Mitch's vision was blurring and blood was
streaming from his mouth. Matt's words
seemed to ring throughout his brain: *Don't be
a quitter, don't be a quitter!* Jason was depend-
ing on him: he couldn't let him down!

Summoning up his last reserves of strength,
Mitch lashed out one final furious blow. It sent
Ruddick splashing back into the water, where
he sank unconscious to the bottom.

There was no time to lose, Mitch realised.
Ruddick would only be out cold for a few
seconds. But a few seconds were exactly what
Mitch needed. He managed to get to the side of
the pool and hauled himself out of the water.
His legs still refusing to move, he pulled himself
over to where the remote control to the chair
had landed when he had knocked it out of Ruddick's hand. Feverishly he stabbed at the controls, and the chair carrying Jason began to rise
slowly out of the water. He lowered the chair
on to the poolside and quickly began to untie
Jason's bonds.

'You OK, Mitch?' Jason asked.

'Yeah,' said Mitch, panting for breath. 'Never
had a better day in my life. How you doin'?'

'I'm doin' fine.'

With an enormous rush of water, Ruddick, who had regained consciousness more quickly than Mitch had bargained for, suddenly sprang out of the water and grabbed Mitch, trying to pull him back into the pool. He failed and the two of them rolled about on the poolside. Ruddick got on top of Mitch and held his head, trying to bring it crashing down on the side of the pool. With all his strength Mitch tried to push him off, but it was all he could do to prevent the crook from smashing his skull wide open on the edge of the pool

Suddenly Ruddick relaxed his hold a little. His revolver was down by Mitch's feet. He reached out for it. Mitch struggled to hold him back. If Ruddick got hold of his gun he would have no compunction in shooting both him and Jason dead in cold blood.

Restrained by Mitch, Ruddick couldn't quite reach the gun. It lay tantalising inches away from his outstretched fingers. He fought wildly to release himself from Mitch's grasp.

Just another inch, and he would be able to reach the weapon.

Just one more inch . . .

Ruddick's fingers closed on the revolver by Mitch's feet –

– and Mitch kicked out at the revolver, send-

ing it splashing into the pool, where it sank
immediately to the bottom.

With a mighty heave Mitch shoved Ruddick
off him just as the doors crashed open and a
team of security guards, led by Sophie, entered
the therapy area. They rushed over to Ruddick
and led him away.

Sophie sped immediately to Jason's side.
'Jason, are you OK? Are you all right?' She was
close to tears.

Jason shrugged her off, and nodded over to
Mitch. 'Mitch saved my life,' he said
proudly.

'Did you, Mitch?' Sophie said and looked at
the drenched lifeguard. 'You know, if you
wanted to take a swim all you had to do was
ask!' she wisecracked.

Jason indicated the revolver lying at the
bottom of the pool.

'He kicked the gun into the pool . . .' Jason's
voice trailed off as he suddenly realised what
he had just said.

He looked at Mitch. Sophie looked at Mitch.
Mitch looked at the revolver he had kicked into
the pool.

That he had *kicked*.

*

'I moved my leg!' he gasped. 'I did! I kicked the gun into the pool!'

'Yes!' cheered Sophie as big tears of joy began to pour out of her eyes.

'I moved my leg!'

'Yes, yes, yes!' Jason was crying now.

'I moved my leg!'

Now Mitch was crying too, and Sophie and Jason came up and hugged him. All three of them were in tears.

*'I moved my leg!'*

# Chapter Fourteen

Mitch looked at his fellow patients at the Rehab Centre who had gathered to bid him goodbye. They had all heard about his rescue of Jason and had come to pay their respects.

Mitch found the whole thing a little embarrassing; which was strange because, down at Baywatch, he would lap up all the adulation accorded to him by the bathing beauties impressed by his latest death-defying rescue.

He was still in his wheelchair, even though it was now less of a necessity and more of a convenience for him. From the moment he had kicked the gun into the pool his progress had been rapid, surprising even the seen-it-all-and-nothing-is-gonna-surprise-me Sophie. The others, he knew, might never be able to leave their wheelchairs for the rest of their life.

*Just like Jason,* he realised, although Jason wasn't among the ones to wave him goodbye. The day after Mitch had saved his life Jason had been taken by the police (the *genuine* article this time) to a safe house, the location of which not even Mitch was allowed to know.

He waved a final goodbye to his farewell committee and headed towards the exit doors which sighed open automatically at his approach. Sophie followed closely behind, no longer bothering to push Mitch's wheelchair. He was strong enough now to get about by himself.

Beyond the doors an ambulance was waiting – the ambulance which would take him back to Baywatch and the world he thought he would never know again. A medical orderly was also waiting for him, holding an aluminium walking frame by his side.

Doctor Zack had assured Mitch that he would soon be up and walking as easily as before his accident; but for the next few weeks he would need the help of the walker.

As soon as he'd passed through the open double doors Mitch made an effort to leave his wheelchair and stand up.

'Mitch! Sit down!' bellowed Sophie, with an authority that would have given even the President of the United States pause for some serious thought.

Mitch promptly sat down again, but shot Stephanie a look which seemed to say: *Hey, what gives? I can walk again now! Why shouldn't I walk outta here and to the car?*

'I can manage now!' he protested.

'Sit down!' she repeated, and glanced over at the other patients, still firmly confined to their wheelchairs and with little hope of ever leaving them: 'It's procedure, Mitch . . .'

Mitch shrugged, imagining how he might feel if he was stuck in a wheelchair and saw someone just up and walk away. Would he be happy for them? Or would he feel another emotion? 'OK . . .'

'And besides,' Sophie added with a lascivious twinkle in her eye, 'don't try to rob me of my last official duty!'

Mitch was puzzled, but let the matter drop.

'Now, it's important that you swim as much as possible, OK?' said Sophie.

Mitch nodded enthusiastically. *Just let anyone try to keep me away from that big, beautiful ocean!* he thought.

'And please keep up your leg exercises,' she continued. 'And not once a day, not twice a day, but –'

Mitch grinned: he'd heard it so many times before that he'd even gotten to repeating it in his sleep. 'I know – "five times a day keeps the pain away"!'

'You got it, honey!'

Mitch looked fondly at Sophie. 'You know,' he admitted, 'I'm gonna miss you . . .'

Sophie smiled and there was a tear in her eye. If she was truthful with herself, she had to admit that all along she had had serious doubts about whether Mitch was ever going to walk again; and yet here he was, all ready to race down to the beach at Baywatch and plunge into the warm and welcoming waters of the great Pacific.

*Never underestimate a Baywatch lifeguard*, she reminded herself. *You never know when they're gonna surprise you!*

'I'm gonna miss you too,' she conceded.

'If it hadn't been for you I wouldn't be walking out of here,' Mitch said. 'I really don't know how to thank you . . .'

'Just to see those buns of yours up and moving is all the thanks I need,' she claimed. 'Now, come on . . . get on up . . . walk away so that I can get a real good look at you . . .'

With Sophie's help Mitch staggered out of his wheelchair and tottered over to the walking frame by the ambulance. His legs still felt weak and painful, but the most important thing was that he could actually *feel* them again, could feel them working and hurting and walking. It was all he could do not to let the emotion show in his face and to hold back the tears which were already welling up in his eyes.

Behind him Sophie beamed with pride and delight. She kept her eyes fixed firmly on Mitch's backside and let out a loud and raucous wolf-whistle.

'Ah yes!' she gushed lewdly, and licked her lips. 'Those buns of yours sure are just something else! Mmmmm-mmmmmmmmmmm!'

Mitch turned around, and looked back at the woman who had repeatedly forced him to go through hell to get him walking again. He grinned affectionately, gratefully, at her. He was never going to forget Sophie for as long as he lived.

'You like what you see?' he laughed.

Sophie grinned back. 'You bet!' she said. 'It sure was well worth the wait, honey! It sure was well worth the wait!'

# Epilogue

The Rehab Centre ambulance had driven Mitch right down to the beach at Baywatch, where he had insisted on getting out without any assistance from the driver or the medical orderly who had accompanied him there.

He stood and looked around him, at the blue Pacific, at the joggers on the shore, the holiday-makers playing beachball on the sand. Soon, Mitch knew, he'd be back there joining in with them.

It felt good to feel the sand beneath his feet once again, feel the sun on his face, and taste the salt-tang of the ocean on his lips. In the distance stood Baywatch headquarters, and, using the walking frame for support, he began to shuffle his way towards it.

The corridors at headquarters were curiously

empty as Mitch walked slowly through them;
he wondered where everyone was. Normally the
place was a hive of activity, with people rushing
back and forth, handing in reports and rushing off on urgent rescue missions. Now, however, it was as quiet as a Sunday morning in
the middle of winter.

Mitch turned the corner into the corridor
which led to his office and the main operations
room, and instantly saw the reason for the
silence and emptiness. The large double doors
to the operations room had been flung open,
and waiting for him there was a large welcoming committee.

The room had been decorated with streamers
and balloons and hung from one wall to the
other was a large banner with the words *Welcome Home Mitch* written across it in brightly-
coloured letters. Stephanie, Hobie, Matt and
CJ, Summer, Ben, Barnett and Newman were
all waiting for him, and as he approached they
gave a huge cheer.

Mitch grinned from ear to ear and shuffled
forwards to greet his friends. It was still difficult walking, even with the aid of the walker,
but Sophie had assured him that as the days
passed walking would get easier and easier
until he was back to normal.

'I don't know why they call these things walkers,' he grumbled good-naturedly, tottering into the operations room. 'It's me who's doin' all the walking!'

Hobie rushed forwards to hug his dad, closely followed by Stephanie, who had just brushed away a tear. Despite all her previous claims that Mitch was going to be all right, in her heart of hearts she had feared that he'd never walk again. It was like a dream come true to see him up and about and back at Baywatch.

'It's great to have you back, Mitch,' she whispered into his ear, and kissed him fondly. Matt, CJ and the others all came over to slap him on the back.

'Yeah,' agreed Matt. 'It was no fun here without you!'

Ben walked forward, leaning on his walking cane for support. 'Good to see you again, big guy.'

Remaining in the background was a portly middle-aged man whom Mitch didn't recognise: by his side, in his wheelchair, was a beaming Jason.

The stranger came up and introduced himself as Detective North, the detective who'd originally been assigned to Jason's case.

'It's good to meet you, at last, Mr Buchannon,' he said, and glanced over at Jason. 'I promised Eddie that I'd bring him back to LA after the trial. We're gonna have some real fun this time, aren't we, Eddie?'

*Eddie?*

Mitch went up to the black lad in his wheelchair and gave him a comradely slap on the shoulder.

'So that's your real name,' he said. 'Eddie ... yeah, I like it ... I heard you beat up those punks real bad in court, huh?'

Jason – or rather Eddie – clapped his hands together in triumph. 'We nailed 'em!' he crowed.

'Thanks to Eddie's testimony, those punks who killed his brother will go down for a long, long time, along with Macieri, their boss, and that turncoat Ruddick,' said North.

'If it wasn't for Mitch I wouldn't have been around to do it,' Eddie pointed out. 'He saved my life.'

Hobie came up to Mitch and Eddie and handed a colourfully wrapped package to Eddie. 'We got something for you,' he said. 'A souvenir from all of us at Baywatch.'

Eddie was amazed. He'd never had any presents before, except from his dead brother. Back home in Chicago there were more important things to think about: like staying alive on the mean streets and having enough money to eat. He quickly ripped off the paper which Stephanie had spent so much time carefully wrapping.

Eddie's eyes widened with amazement as he saw what the gang at Baywatch had clubbed together to buy him. Sealed in a Perspex case so that it would remain undamaged for ever, was a baseball card of Ted Williams, in perfect condition and signed by the great baseball hero himself.

'Wow, this is something else!' he marvelled, and then looked up at Mitch. 'Thanks, Mitch, I'll never forget you.'

Mitch took off the young boy's baseball cap and ruffled his hair. 'And I'm never gonna forget you either,' he said. 'I'll come visit you, OK?'

'OK.'

Ben came up to Mitch, leaning on his cane for support. 'You know, Mitch,' he said. 'I think that it's about time that you took me up on that offer.'

Mitch frowned. 'And what offer might that be?' he asked.

'Our race – remember?' he grinned. 'Come on!'

And without further ado Ben raced off out of the doors, the sound of his walking cane clip-clopping on the floor.

'Hey! Come back!' cried Mitch and, with his walking frame, shuffled off in hot pursuit.

As the two men disappeared down the corridor Stephanie laughed and took Hobie in her arms. She kissed him fondly.

The old Mitch had returned, they both realised. The walking Mitch, the Mitch who would face up to any challenge life might throw at him, the Mitch they all depended on, the Mitch who took life as it came, the Mitch who never took anything seriously apart from the welfare of his buddies, saving people's lives, and the great beach and ocean outside.

For Mitch was the very spirit of the Los Angeles County Lifeguards. And without Mitch Buchannon and men and women like him there would be no Baywatch.

And it was good to have him back!

Join the **BAYWATCHERS FAN NETWORK** now and keep in touch with your favourite Baywatch stars and all the latest Baywatch news.

For further information please send a large s.a.e. to:

**BAYWATCHERS FAN NETWORK**
**PO BOX 1443**
**POOLE**
**DORSET**
**BH15 3YP**

# BAYWATCH™

# THE DEVIL'S MOUTH

At Baywatch headquarters, rookie lifeguards are lining up on Malibu Beach for the gruelling annual qualifying swim... But who will make the grade?

Meanwhile, Mitch sets off for California's gold country when he learns that his eccentric uncle has drowned while hunting for a legendary gold nugget. The search for his missing body leads to a stretch of treacherous rapids... and a whole lot of trouble!

ISBN 1–85283–847–7

**£2.99**